## "Cora can teach in my stead until I'm healed enough to return to work."

"I'll take good care of your students while you're on the mend," she promised. "And I'll be sure they stay on task with their studies."

"Of course you will," Tobit said, still unsmiling. "Because you'll be doing as I direct every step of the way."

Cora stared at him. "As you *direct*?"

Her uncle moved close. "We were just discussing how it would work. Tobit will continue writing the lesson plans and he'll grade the papers."

Cora's face fell. Tobit was going to write the lesson plans and grade papers for her? That didn't make her a teacher at all. It made her a... *babysitter*. "Whose idea was that?" she blurted.

Uncle Cyrus's forehead creased. "Whose idea was what?"

"To...to have him oversee my job," she sputtered. "To tell me what to do."

"Me," Tobit said from his bed. "And you'll do as I instruct," Tobit continued, meeting her gaze without flinching. "Or we'll find someone else."

**Emma Miller** lives quietly in her old farmhouse in rural Delaware. Fortunate enough to have been born into a family of strong faith, she grew up on a dairy farm, surrounded by loving parents, siblings, grandparents, aunts, uncles and cousins. Emma was educated in local schools and once taught in an Amish schoolhouse. When she's not caring for her large family, reading and writing are her favorite pastimes.

### Books by Emma Miller

### Love Inspired

#### *Seven Amish Sisters*

*Her Surprise Christmas Courtship*
*Falling for the Amish Bad Boy*
*The Teacher's Christmas Secret*

*The Amish Spinster's Courtship*
*The Christmas Courtship*
*A Summer Amish Courtship*
*An Amish Holiday Courtship*
*Courting His Amish Wife*
*Their Secret Courtship*

Visit the Author Profile page at LoveInspired.com for more titles.

# The Teacher's Christmas Secret

## Emma Miller

**LOVE INSPIRED**

INSPIRATIONAL ROMANCE

LOVE INSPIRED®
INSPIRATIONAL ROMANCE

Recycling programs for this product may not exist in your area.

ISBN-13: 978-1-335-59690-1

The Teacher's Christmas Secret

Copyright © 2023 by Emma Miller

For questions and comments about the quality of this book, please contact us at CustomerService@Harlequin.com.

Love Inspired
22 Adelaide St. West, 41st Floor
Toronto, Ontario M5H 4E3, Canada
www.LoveInspired.com

Printed in U.S.A.

Whoso findeth a wife findeth a good thing,
and obtaineth favour of the Lord.
—*Proverbs* 18:22

# Chapter One

*Autumn*
*Honeycomb, Delaware*

Cora Koffman carried a tray of homemade cookies from the commercial kitchen to the sales floor of her family's Amish country store. "This is the last of Annie Chupp's cookies," she called to her youngest sister, who stood behind the checkout counter. It would be an hour before they opened the shop, but they had a list of tasks to complete before the first customers of the day walked through the door.

"Already out?" Jane looked up as she slid a stack of dollar bills into the cash register. "But she just brought them yesterday."

Cora set the tray of bagged cookies on the display table. "I don't know what to tell you. Annie makes good cookies? The chocolate peanut butter and the butter-scotch blondies are all gone." She surveyed the tray. "Only gingersnaps, double-chocolate brownies and lemon spritz left."

Jane pushed the cash drawer closed on the register. "We had three customers yesterday asking for Annie's cookies. One Englisher wanted to know if she could order eight dozen for a luncheon she's having on Saturday." She tapped her fingers thoughtfully on the polished wood countertop. "Do you think Annie would be willing to do that?"

"I guess you'll have to ask her," Cora answered, sounding sharper than intended. She stopped what she was doing and breathed deeply, exhaling before she spoke in a gentler tone. "I'm sorry. I didn't mean to be short with you."

"It's *oll recht, schweschter.*" Jane came out from behind the counter to help Cora place the bags of cookies in the display baskets. "I know you don't want to work here."

Cora pressed her hand to her forehead. "It's not that. This is a family business and we all have to pitch in so we can see *Dat* well cared for. We agreed to that when we built it. And with Millie and Beth gone on their honeymoons, I know we're shorthanded."

"*Ya*, we are. Especially since Henry is hopeless when it comes to inside work, unless it's repairing or building something," Jane pointed out. "Yesterday I asked her to keep an eye on the front counter while I went into the back to see if we had any more of my blackberry jam to sell. In the five minutes I was gone, she'd rung up a customer wrong and managed to lock down the register."

Cora chuckled. Their sister Henrietta, whom they called Henry, did the maintenance on their farm, which with their father suffering from early-onset Alzheimer's, was a Godsend. She even occasionally made money doing handiwork for Amish and English widows. After losing their mother two years ago, and with their father's inability to work any longer, the seven sisters had been forced to figure out how to bring income into the household any way they could. They'd built the store on their property for that reason, and it was turning out to be a profitable endeavor, to the surprise of the family and the Amish community of Honeycomb.

"It's not that I don't want to help," Cora explained. "It's only that I really wanted that teaching job. I still can't believe they gave it to someone else. To an outsider, no less." Her words sounded bitter and she didn't want to be that way. Every night she prayed to *Gott* to help her see beyond her anger and resentment and remember that He always has a plan for his faithful.

"And they hired another *man*." Jane frowned, planting her hands on her hips. "All that talk about it was high time we hired a single woman like other Amish communities and they hire a man anyway." She shook her head. "And *that* man. Tobit Lapp. He's not even *from* here. Why did the school board hire him?"

"I don't know. Maybe they felt sorry for him," Cora answered. "Him being a widower raising a son on his own."

Jane made a face. "He looks like a big bear and Charlie says he's mean as one. Last week he made the poor boy stay in for recess because he hadn't finished his reading worksheet." She pursed her lips. "Everyone knows Charlie doesn't have a head for reading."

Charlie was their new brother-in-law Jack's twelve-year-old sibling. After issues at home with their father, Charlie had moved in with Jack in the apartment above the store. When Jack and Beth returned from their honeymoon, the new couple would live there until they built a house. Where Charlie would live then hadn't been decided. Their oldest sister Eleanor's opinion was that Charlie was getting on so well living in the main house with them that he ought to remain there when the newlyweds returned home. According to Eleanor, no bride should have to start married life sharing her first home with anyone's little brother.

"I told Jack when he called the other day to check on things that I'd speak with Tobit about Charlie," Cora said. "That man has no right to pick on him the way he does and I'd tell him so."

Jane's eyes widened. "You wouldn't!"

"I most certainly would. And while I was at it, I'd tell him to stop sending so much schoolwork home. A boy Charlie's age has chores to do after school." Cora crossed her arms, irritated by the mere thought of Tobit Lapp. "Supposedly he's had years of teaching experience in Indiana and Ohio, but I'm not sure I believe it. Someone with *years* of experience ought to know that boys Charlie's age shouldn't have homework."

"*Ya*, you'd think he'd know that," Jane chimed in. "Especially when his son, Elijah, is the same age as Charlie. Both are sixth graders." Something caught her eye and she leaned to see around Cora. Her forehead creased. "Speaking of Charlie." She strode toward the front door with a Closed sign hanging from it.

Cora turned around to see what her sister saw— Charlie cutting across the empty parking lot toward them, swinging his lunch pail.

Jane unlocked the front door and waited for the boy

as he walked up the porch steps. "Don't tell me Teacher sent you home for bad behavior again," she said.

"That's it," Cora fumed, striding toward the door. "Jack might be too busy to talk to that man, but I'm not. I'm going to that school and talking to Tobit right this minute."

"*Nay*, I wasn't bad," Charlie protested. "We all got sent home."

"Why?" Cora asked, stepping back as Jane let him in the door.

"Teacher wasn't there," Charlie answered excitedly. He was the spitting image of his big brother Jack with shaggy blond hair and blue eyes. All the Koffman sisters agreed that Charlie would be every bit as handsome as his brother once he was out of the gangly stage all boys his age went through. "Teacher sent Elijah to tell us there was no school today and likely no school the rest of the week. Elijah said that in all the confusion yesterday, his *dat* forgot to send out word."

"Send out word of what?" Cora closed the door behind the boy and locked it.

"That there's no school!" Charlie answered. "Elijah said there's likely no school for days while the school board figures things out. You think they'll just cancel school until after Christmas?"

"I seriously doubt that," Jane told him. "Christmas is two months off."

"Back to school being canceled." Her hand on her hip, Cora narrowed her gaze. "*Why* is there no school?"

Charlie gestured impatiently. "Because Teacher fell and broke his leg. Here." He tapped below his knee.

"It's bad. He broke his—what's this bone called?" He pointed below his knee.

"Tibia, I think," Cora said.

"*Ya,* his tibia. He had to have surgery last night. Elijah said his *dat* was supposed to stay in the hospital but he said no because he didn't want Elijah home alone and he didn't want to ask anyone to keep him. An ambulance brought Teacher home this morning. And they might get a fancy bed for their parlor because Teacher's not supposed to climb stairs so he can't get to his bedroom."

"Oh my goodness." Jane pressed her hand to her mouth. "How did Tobit break his leg?"

Charlie set his tin lunch pail on a display rack of horse liniment. "Is it okay if I eat my lunch?" He flipped open the metal lid. "Eleanor made me a peanut butter and marshmallow fluff sandwich. She said I wasn't to eat it on my way to school again but to save it for lunch." He plucked the sandwich wrapped in beeswax fabric from the box and held it up. "But since I'm not having lunch at school today—"

"Charlie," Cora interrupted, a plan forming in her head. She certainly wouldn't want to take advantage of anyone's injury, but if Tobit was hurt and couldn't work, the school would need a new teacher. According to Jack, whose oldest brother was on the school board that oversaw all the one-room Amish schoolhouses in Honeycomb, she and Tobit had been the finalists in the job search. It would only be logical if they had to replace a teacher quickly, she would be the best choice.

"Charlie," Cora repeated, resting her hand on his shoulder. The boy was already as tall as she was, but that wasn't saying much. She was the shortest of the seven Koffman girls at barely five feet tall. "How did Teacher break his leg?"

"Fell from his windmill."

Jane gasped. "What was he doing on his windmill?"

Charlie unwrapped his sandwich and took a big bite. "Repairing it," he answered, his mouth full. "Elijah said he was feeding the chickens when he heard his father holler. Elijah ran around the barn and his father was just laying there."

"Lying," Cora corrected.

Charlie looked at her quizzically. "*Nay*, no one lied."

"The correct use of the word is that Tobit was *lying* there. Not laying. Hens lay."

Charlie bit off another piece of sandwich. "Elijah said he thought his *dat* was dead. But he wasn't. But his leg is busted up bad. The doctor had to put metal screws and stuff in it."

"And you say Tobit is home now?" Cora asked.

Charlie chewed noisily. *"Ya."*

Cora spun around to her sister. "Was that your home-made chicken noodle soup I saw in the refrigerator in the back?"

*"Ya,"* Jane said. "It's for our lunch. Why?"

"I think I'll pay poor Tobit Lapp a visit and take him some soup," Cora said. "And some cookies." She grabbed Charlie's lunch box, dropped several bags of Annie's cookies into it and strode toward the back rooms, the box in hand. "I'll pay for them later. Be back as quick as I can, Jane!"

"Hey," Charlie cried, jogging after her. "That's my lunch box!"

* * *

Twenty minutes later, Cora eased the family buggy to a stop at a crossroad. It was a crisp, cool day but the sun was shining, and she was plenty warm in knitted fingerless gloves and the denim barn jacket one of her sisters had recently made for her.

She looked both ways and then turned off their street, Plum Tree Road, and onto Clover Road. Tobit Lapp and his son lived half a mile past the Amish school Charlie attended. She gave their driving horse a bit of rein and glanced at Charlie sitting beside her. "Why again are you going with me?" she asked, half teasing.

"I told you. To keep an eye on my lunch pail." He pointed to the large, domed lunch box on the seat between them. "Eleanor said that if I lost another, I'd be carrying a paper sack to school. The kids will make fun of me."

Inside the pail were the bags of cookies and the jar of Jane's homemade soup that her little sister had intended for their lunch. Charlie's potato chips and apple were still inside, but she'd promised the boy she wouldn't give them to his teacher.

"Also, to watch the fireworks," Charlie added.

"What fireworks?" Cora drew back. "I'm taking lunch to a neighbor who's feeling poorly."

"I think you're going to tell Teacher that you want his job." Charlie beamed. "I'd love it if you were my teacher. I bet you'd never make me do my multiplication tables."

She cut her eyes at him. "You'd be wrong about that. Everyone needs to know how to multiply, Charlie. And if you'd apply yourself, I know you could learn them.

But you have to keep using the flashcards I made for you. You're in sixth grade now. You should know multiplication so you can divide."

He frowned and stared ahead. "I'd rather quit school. I could work at the store. I could stock shelves, sweep, mow the lawn, whatever you need."

"You are not quitting school," she responded firmly.

"My father quit after the fourth grade," the boy countered.

Cora could think of several responses to that statement, but none would have been kind. While she didn't care for Sharar Lehman and his heavy-handedness when he disciplined his children, the man was still Charlie and Jack's father and for that, he was due respect. "This is Tobit's place coming up, isn't it?" she asked instead. She knew it was. Every time she passed it, she stewed over the fact that Tobit got the job that should have been hers.

*"Ya."* Charlie craned his neck as they turned into the lane. This property was small, only ten acres, perhaps, with a well-kept white-clapboard bungalow and ample outbuildings. Because Tobit didn't farm for a living, the place was the perfect size to have room for his livestock, a substantial garden and to grow a few acres of crops for his animals. As the barnyard came into view, she spotted four buggies and recognized the buggy belonging to her uncle, their family's bishop.

"Looks like others had the same idea we had," Cora said.

"Bet nobody else stole someone's lunch pail," Charlie grumbled.

Cora eased the buggy between two others at a hitching rail in front of a newly painted chicken house. "I did not steal it. I *borrowed* it."

"If you say so." They rolled to a stop and Charlie jumped down to secure the driving horse to the hitching rail.

"I say so," Cora murmured under her breath. Now that she was here, she was nervous and wondered if it had been a mistake to come. But then she realized that the other buggies all belonged to men on the school board. That likely meant they were trying to figure out what they were going to do about finding another teacher.

Perhaps *Gott* intended for her to be here at this moment.

She reached into the buggy, grabbed Charlie's lunch box and strode across the driveway toward the house. As she walked, she smoothed her prayer *kapp*, thankful she had put on a new tab dress and fresh white apron that morning. Dressed as she was, neither her uncle nor the school board members would be able to find fault with her appropriately plain appearance. She looked the part of a schoolteacher and she knew she would make a good one. All she had to do was convince their bishop and the school board members.

Tobit's opinion, she decided as she walked briskly up to the front porch, was inconsequential. These men served on the board that had hired him, which meant they had the authority to hire her. When she reached the door, which was also freshly painted, she glanced over her shoulder, looking for Charlie. He stood near the barn, head down, scuffing one boot in the gravel as he talked to Tobit's son.

*Good,* she thought. She didn't expect *fireworks*, but she saw no need to have Charlie or Elijah witness Tobit making a fool of himself in protest of being replaced by her. She hoped he wouldn't, but it was her experience that men rarely liked being reminded that women could do most of the things men could.

Cora took a deep breath to calm her nerves and knocked on the door. To her surprise, her aunt opened it.

"Aunt Judy," Cora said, not sure why it hadn't occurred to her that she might be there. Of course Judy would have accompanied her husband, the bishop, to call on an injured member of their community.

"Cora." Judy smiled as she dried her hands on her apron.

"Jack's brother Charlie told us what happened to Tobit and I came right away," Cora explained. "Jane sent chicken soup. Is the injury bad?"

"Terrible," her mother's sister said, lowering her voice as she glanced over her shoulder. "It's a wonder he survived."

From behind her aunt, Cora heard several male voices. She couldn't make out what they were saying, but their tones made it clear that they were having a serious conversation.

"Tobit ought to be in the hospital," Judy whispered. "With no wife or older daughters, who's going to care for him? He says he and his boy make out just fine, but what do men know about caring for the sick?" She stepped back, opening the door farther. "Come in. I'm sure Tobit will be pleased to see you."

*Not when he hears what I have to say,* Cora thought. But she kept the comment to herself. Instead, she said,

"I see that Jim Mast, Matt Beachy and Junior Yoder are here. All members of the school board." Jack's brother was missing, but she knew he was out of town attending a wedding in the Midwest.

"*Ya.* They're trying to decide what's to be done," Judy whispered, closing the door behind Cora. "Give me your jacket." She put out her hand. "The doctor says at least a month of bed rest if Tobit wants to walk normally again. And even then he won't be able to work for another month."

"What do you mean *what's to be done*?" Cora asked as she handed over the lunch box and her denim jacket.

"About school, of course." Judy took the items from her. "The children can't go months without their studies and no family is going to like the idea of sending their children to other schools farther from their homes. Cyrus says that's not a good solution anyway because we're already at capacity at the other schools in Honeycomb. The poor things won't even have desks."

"*Ach*, that is a problem, isn't it?" Cora said. "But maybe I can help."

Judy grasped Cora's hand. She was a tall, broad-shouldered woman with an iron grip. "That's what I told Cyrus. And now here you are, showing up so timely on Tobit's doorstep." She led Cora through the front hall. The little house was neat as a pin and surprisingly cozy. "They're in the parlor." She pointed in the direction the voices were coming from.

Cora hesitated, wondering if this was the right thing to do. If the men were gathered to discuss replacing the teacher, would it be wiser for her to join Judy in the kitchen and wait for them to come to her? She knew that her uncle was the kind of man who liked to think any good idea was his own. Maybe the other school board members were the same way and wouldn't appreciate her asking for the job. Maybe she should let them offer it to her.

But Cora couldn't take the chance of losing this opportunity. At her age, she would soon have to start thinking about marriage. And once she wed and had a family to care for, she wouldn't be able to teach. So it was now or never.

Before she could chicken out, Cora threw back her shoulders, stood as tall as possible and walked into the parlor. The first thing she saw was Tobit lying in a hospital bed. As Jane had pointed out, he was a big bear of a man—a foot taller than Cora with muscular shoulders that always seemed barely contained by his shirt. He had hair so dark that it was almost black and he needed a haircut. He wasn't what she would have called a handsome man, but he had intense blue eyes that immediately drew her in. When Tobit made eye contact with her, she had to force herself to look away.

Her uncle was the next to notice her. "Cora," he said.

"Bishop." She nodded to her uncle and then in the direction of the other men. "Jim, Matt, Junior."

The men all looked surprised to see her.

Cora shifted her gaze to the man in the bed again. Tobit had a bedsheet drawn up to his waist but was wearing a blue shirt, which was a relief. It hadn't occurred to her that a man as severely injured as Tobit might have been wearing bedclothes. It would have been inappropriate for her, as a single woman, to call on a single man in bedclothes.

"I... I'm Cora Koffman," she told Tobit, unsure why she was so nervous. "We've met before. Charlie Lehman is staying with my family while his brother, our brother-in-law, is on his honeymoon."

Tobit was silent long enough to make her uncomfortable. Then in a deep voice, he said, "I remember you, Cora." He didn't smile.

"I'm... I was sorry—*we* were sorry to hear about your injury. My family and I will pray for a swift and full recovery. I brought you some chicken soup." She lamely indicated the direction of the kitchen. "My sister Jane made the noodles—the soup." She suddenly felt so tongue-tied that she wasn't sure she could go on. But she had to.

Cora turned to the other men. "I came to volunteer to teach the children at our Clover school. Until Tobit can return to the position. I can teach the whole year if need be," she added, her back now to Tobit.

"See." Junior, who was as wide as tall and ruddy faced, raised his hand and indicated Cora. "I told you she was our best option. And *Gott* has brought her to us."

Cora's eyes widened, a smile tugging on the corners of her mouth. "You'd consider hiring me?"

Her Uncle Cyrus looked from her to the other school board members. "What do you think?"

"Ask the teacher. It's his school. His students," Jim Mast said.

Matt Beachy nodded. "I agree." He pointed to the bed. "Ask Teacher."

"What say you?" Bishop Cyrus asked, turning to Tobit.

*"Ya,"* Tobit responded. "Cora can teach in my stead until I'm healed enough to return to work."

Cora turned to look at the newcomer, a smile crossing her face. "I'll take good care of your students while you're on the mend," she promised. "And I'll be sure they stay on task with their studies."

"Of course you will," Tobit said, still unsmiling. "Because you'll be doing as I direct every step of the way."

Cora stared at him. "As you *direct*?"

"I'm so glad you're willing to fill in for Tobit on such short notice." Her uncle moved close. "We were just discussing how it would work. Tobit will continue writing the lesson plans and he'll grade the papers."

Cora's face fell. Tobit was going to write the lesson plans and grade papers for her? That didn't make her a teacher at all. It made her a…*babysitter*. "Whose idea was that?" she blurted.

Her Uncle Cyrus's leather forehead creased. "Whose idea was what?"

She dropped her hand to her hips. "To have him…" She was so angry she couldn't find the words to express herself. "To…to have him oversee my job," she sputtered. "To tell me what to do."

"Me," Tobit said from his bed.

Cora looked at him.

"And you'll do as I instruct," Tobit continued, meeting her gaze without flinching. "Or we'll find someone else."

# Chapter Two

Cora's sister Willa scooped lima beans seasoned with bacon into a serving dish. "I can't believe you went to his house, *schweschter*." Her brown eyes were wide with awe. A year younger than Cora, she was the prettiest of the Koffman sisters and the envy of every unwed Amish girl in Honeycomb. All the bachelors doted on her. "Tobit is so big and—" She searched for the right word.

"Scary," Jane finished for her as she carried a plate of garlic-roasted chicken to the kitchen table.

"Mean," Charlie suggested as he set the last utensils in place on the table.

Eleanor shot a warning glance at the boy as, with a quart-size canning jar in each hand, she closed the refrigerator door with her hip. "I won't have you speaking disrespectfully about your teacher, Charlie." She set the jars of chow-chow and fresh applesauce on the table. "I told you that the other day. I understand that the two of you butt heads, but we need to learn to get along with anyone and everyone."

Charlie nodded and lowered his gaze, seeming properly chastised but his half smile was mischievous. Cora liked that in him. She had a feeling it was his spirit that had helped him survive in his father's abusive household.

"Jane is right. Tobit Lapp is scary," Willa agreed. "I ran into him and his boy at Spence's Bazaar last week and he barely spoke when I greeted them. It was more like a…growl." She shuddered.

Cora carried a serving bowl of steaming-hot buttery mashed potatoes to the table, refusing to voice the fact that she found Tobit scary, too. If she was going to work with him…*for* him, she would have to get over that. If she didn't, his intimidation might affect her ability to teach the children of Honeycomb effectively.

"Exactly," Jane agreed as she added a serving spoon to the lima beans before bringing them to the table. "He doesn't speak. He just growls. And he's so big." She set the bowl down. "But he's still a member of our community. I'm making beef stew in the morning to send over to Tobit and his son. I'll make plenty so we can have it for our supper tomorrow night, too."

"I love your beef stew," Charlie piped up. "Can we have biscuits?"

Jane smiled at the boy who had found his way into their home through his brother but into their hearts all on his own. "Cheesy biscuits or buttermilk?"

Charlie beamed. "Buttermilk, please."

"Did anyone tell *Dat* that supper was ready?" Eleanor moved a fork from one side of a dinner plate to the other. "Fork on the left, knife on the right, Charlie."

Charlie glanced down at another place setting and quickly switched the fork and the knife. "Felty's still in the parlor. I told him it was suppertime, but he said he was busy giving Samson a talking-to about his behavior and I wasn't to bother them."

Eleanor exhaled loudly, suggesting it had been a long day with their father. Each of the sisters tried to take turns looking after him so that the responsibility didn't fall solely on their eldest sister's shoulders. However, with Millie and Beth on their honeymoons, and the store being so busy, it didn't always happen.

"Could you fetch him for me, Charlie?" Eleanor gave the boy's shoulder a gentle squeeze of affection.

*"Ya."*

"And be sure he washes his hands after playing with that dog," Eleanor called. As he left the kitchen, she said softly, "I know it was the right thing to take Elden's dog and Jack's brother in while they and the girls are gone, but honestly, the dog is more trouble than the boy." Elden, like Jack, was their new brother-in-law.

Cora smiled to herself. Eleanor, who had taken charge of the household when their mother died, liked to put on a tough, no-nonsense air, but she was one of the kindest people Cora had ever known. Eleanor had insisted on taking the dog and Charlie into their home so the newly married couples could have some time to themselves before they began the daily routines of married life.

Cora suspected that while Eleanor might not admit it, she was enjoying the little bit of mothering that Charlie needed. With Jane, the youngest in the family, at seventeen, she neither needed nor welcomed Eleanor fussing over her, so it was nice that their eldest sister could steer her nurturing in another direction. This was especially true because Eleanor believed that because she'd had a foot amputated as a child, she would never marry. Her whole life centered on the Koffman farm and her family and she had no dreams of a husband and children of her own. It didn't matter how hard their parents or now her sisters tried to convince her that no one noticed the prosthetic beneath her long skirt. It certainly wouldn't matter with the right man, but Eleanor was determined she would remain on their farm and care for their father when her sisters flew from the nest.

"It's going to be hard for *Dat* to let Samson go when Elden and Millie return," Cora said. "He really wants a dog of his own."

"No dog," Eleanor said firmly. Much to their father's chagrin, since the death of their family dog, there hadn't been one on the property. He kept telling anyone who would listen that every Amish farm had to have a dog. So far, Eleanor hadn't relented. "A dog is too big a responsibility for our *vader* now and we all know so."

Cora wasn't sure that she did *know so*. She thought a dog might be good for their *dat*. A little responsibility and something to do with his time might keep him out of mischief. However, she wasn't up for that argument tonight. She had bigger problems on her mind, namely what she was going to do about the teaching position. When she had gone to Tobit's house with the intention of securing the job, it hadn't occurred to her that the man would expect her to work for *him*. How could the school board, men she had known since she was a babe, do that to her? An even bigger question was what was she going to do about it?

A fractured tibia or not, she couldn't work with that man.

But did she have a choice? She had offered to teach while Tobit was laid up. She would have offered to do it for any teacher from the schoolhouses in Honeycomb. Even if another Amish community in the county had needed her, she would have gone. But none of the other teachers were Tobit. None had ridden into town and taken the job that had been meant for her. Tobit, a stranger, had done that.

Then there was the topic of pay. She hadn't thought that through before charging down the road and laying herself open to be used by the stranger. She wasn't sure if she would have demanded to be paid, taking Tobit's salary from him, had the circumstances been different. He was, after all, the head of a household and had no other income. With her family's general store doing so well, their financial burdens had been eased. In fact, Eleanor had recently reported that they were doing so well that their new income wasn't just paying all the bills, there was money to spare. They were able to donate more to their community to cover others' medical costs, a funeral or whatever was needed, but they also now had a healthy savings cushion.

But Cora couldn't work for that man without even being paid. Could she?

"What are you going to do?"

Startled, Cora looked up. It was Jane.

"Do?" Cora asked.

Jane rolled her eyes and set the butter crock on the table, just out of reach of where their father would sit. In the last few weeks, he'd taken to eating butter. Not on bread, but straight out of the crock. And if there was no butter out, he'd snitch it from the refrigerator and hide in the pantry to eat it. And as one would expect, it had not been good for his digestive system.

"About the job," Jane said impatiently. "Are you going to tell the school board you won't work with that man?"

"Jane, stop pestering her," Eleanor chastised. "Cora offered to teach in Tobit's place, not teach under his direction. She'll tell that to the school board, and they'll find someone else. Cora said they all agreed that classes would be suspended until next week. The board can find someone by then, or one of the school board members can do it. It wouldn't be the first time one of them has had to substitute-teach." She smiled kindly at Cora. "It wasn't meant to be, I suppose."

Glancing away from her sisters, Cora gritted her teeth. Eleanor had been opposed to her teaching school from the beginning, even before Cora had applied for the position that Tobit was given. It was Eleanor's opinion that it was time Cora found a husband, got married and started having babies. She was, after all, older than Beth and Millie and now they were married.

But Cora didn't want to get married. Not yet. She wanted to teach school. It had been her dream since she was a little girl in Elmer Krupp's one-room schoolhouse. And Elmer, who was now elderly and blind, had encouraged her, suggesting that even though she was a girl in an Old Order church, she could still strive to be a teacher. He had told her that plenty of single women taught school in other Amish communities in their county and all over the country.

"It's all right, *schweschter*." Eleanor stroked Cora's arm. "You can pay Jim Mast a visit tomorrow and tell him straight out that you won't be teaching at the Clover Road school. You don't even have to give a reason if you don't want to. Or you can blame it on me. You can say I preferred you stayed home to help run the store and care for our father. No one will think any less of you for that."

The matter obviously closed in Eleanor's eyes, she walked away from Cora. "Who else are we missing besides *Dat*?" Eleanor glanced around the kitchen, frowning. "Henry. Where's Henry?"

Willa snitched a crumb of biscuit off the serving plate on the table and popped it into her mouth. "Still not home. Leaky roof on some English lady's trailer house. She called the store as we were locking up. Said she'd be home as soon as she could."

Their sister Henry did work around the house for the widowed and elderly in their community. But she also occasionally worked for Englishers. It was amazing to them all that there was such unconventional work available to a young Amish woman. But it made perfect sense. Many women these days, Amish or English, weren't comfortable having a strange man in their homes.

Eleanor frowned. "I wish she wouldn't stay out so late. I worry about her being on the road after dark. Last month there was that buggy accident with that family from Seven Poplars. It was a wonder no one was more seriously injured."

"She said she was almost done when she called. I expect she'll be here anytime now," Willa said, trying to alleviate her sister's concern.

Their *dat* walked into the kitchen, followed by Charlie and a little mixed-breed bulldog. "Are we going to eat breakfast or not?" the older man demanded impatiently.

Cora and Eleanor both glanced at their father, then at each other. Neither corrected him.

Eleanor took Cora's hand. "Just tell them no and be done with it." She squeezed her hand and released it, turning to their father. "Samson can't come to the supper table, *Dat*. He'll have to go out on the porch."

"It's too cold on the porch," he protested as Jane pulled out his chair at the head of the table and he sat down. "You wouldn't put me out on the porch for breakfast, would you?"

Eleanor rested her hand on her hip. "Fine. But he cannot sit under the table again and beg for food." She pointed to the entrance to the mudroom that led outside. "Samson. Go."

The black-and-white-spotted bulldog obeyed.

"Sit," she instructed, motioning with her hand.

Samson dropped to the floor and their father giggled with delight. "Such a good dog. Well-mannered. I taught him well." He gazed over the table heavily laden with the simple but abundant evening meal. "Do we have any butter? I don't see butter."

The sisters all smiled at each other and then Eleanor turned to Cora. "Tell the school board tomorrow that you won't be working for Tobit and put this behind you. You'll feel better once you do."

Cora said nothing as she watched her sisters take their seats at the family table. Eleanor said she would feel better when she turned down the job, but would she? Cora thought not. She had dreamed of teaching school since she was six and she couldn't let that dream go. Not even for her sister, whom she loved dearly.

And certainly not for the likes of Tobit Lapp.

Tobit tucked a cloth napkin into his shirt beneath his chin and slid the bowl of hot stew closer on the tray on his lap. The smell of the hearty beef and freshly baked, buttery biscuits on a small plate beside the bowl made him realize how hungry he was. It had been two days since he'd eaten anything substantial. The day he fell, his lunch had been a peanut butter and grape jam sandwich on pumpernickel—because that was all he could find in their pantry—eaten at his school desk. He'd fallen from the windmill before he could make supper for himself and his son. Then he'd been too nauseous the previous day to have anything but the broth the bishop's wife had made him the day before and a couple of bites of chicken soup Elijah had found in the fridge. Tobit didn't remember who had left it for him: he'd had several visits from well-meaning neighbors. Most of today he still hadn't felt like eating. But the anesthesia must have finally worn off because suddenly he was hungry enough to eat all the beef stew as well as the pottery bowl it was in.

Tobit glanced up at Elden Yoder, the first friend he'd made in Honeycomb. The first he'd made in years. "You shouldn't have come home early from your honeymoon for me," he said. "I'm fine."

Elden crossed his arms over his chest. "You don't look fine to me. You look like a man who fell twenty-five feet from his windmill and nearly broke his neck."

Unable to stand the tantalizing scent of the food a

moment longer, Tobit scooped up a measure of chunky stew in his spoon and shoveled it into his mouth. When he could speak again, he said, "I didn't break my neck. Just my leg."

"It was a good thing *Gott* was with you and Elijah knew what to do in an emergency. I'm impressed that you have a cell phone and that you taught your boy how to call 911."

Tobit took another bite of stew. It was even more delicious tasting than it smelled, if that was possible. It had been a long time since he'd had homemade beef stew. The only stew he and Elijah ever ate was what came out of a can. Mostly they ate breakfast foods morning and night. Eggs every way you could imagine: fried, scrambled, boiled, poached and in an omelet. He made bacon, scrapple and sausage, and occasionally they had ham and eggs or steak and eggs. On Friday nights they had pancakes, a treat he and his son looked forward to each week.

Tobit reached for one of three buttered buttermilk biscuits that Elden's wife, Millie, had made. She was still in his kitchen. He didn't know what she was doing now, but he had no complaint. She'd brought the stew to reheat and made the biscuits, and his whole house, for the first time since he and Elijah arrived in Honeycomb three months ago, smelled of freshly baked biscuits. The only biscuit he ever made came from a cardboard tube in the refrigerator section of Walmart.

"It's kind of you to be concerned but I'm fine." Tobit opened his arms wide, the biscuit in one hand. "A few days of rest and I'll be as good as new."

As Tobit spoke, Elden's new wife walked into the

parlor-turned-sick-room carrying a jug of fresh milk in one hand and a glass in the other. "Your boy's milked your cow, cleaned the horse stalls and fed and watered the chickens. He's having something to eat now, but when he's done, he'll go back out and take care of the rest of the livestock. Milk?" She held up the jug.

Tobit nodded and reached for his spoon again. He wasn't used to having women around and their presence made him feel awkward. But he liked Millie. He'd liked her the first time he met her. She was round and rosy-cheeked and always had a smile on her face. Elden was a blessed man to have found such a wife, and from across the road from him, no less.

"*Ya*, I'll have some. *Danki*." Tobit dug in for another spoonful of stew. It was the best he'd ever eaten though he didn't know if it was because of the subtle rosemary flavor or because he hadn't eaten in so long. "But there's no need for you to fuss over me like this. I was just telling Elden that you shouldn't have to return early from your honeymoon because of me."

"You saying you wouldn't have done the same for me?" Elden teased.

Millie laughed as she poured the glass nearly to the brim. "Pay no attention to him," she instructed. "He used your injury as an excuse to come home." She shot her husband a glance, her smile mischievous. "Truth is, he missed his dog."

Elden laughed with her and it was obvious there was some private joke between them. Seeing the unspoken exchange, Tobit felt the slightest twinge of envy. He liked watching these two together. It was obvious that not only were they in love, but they genuinely liked each other. Tobit had never been so blessed.

The marriage between him and Elijah's mother, Aida, had been arranged by her parents and the aunt and uncle who had raised Tobit. He and Aida had been compatible enough, or so he had thought at the time. But Aida had never looked at him the way Millie looked at Elden now. The love for each other in their eyes was undeniable.

Tobit glanced down at his supper tray, feeling embarrassed to witness such joy between the newlyweds. Embarrassed to be having these feelings at all. He wasn't that kind of man. He tried not to be self-reflective, and he avoided *getting in touch with his feelings* whenever possible.

Tobit cleared his throat and took a big gulp of the milk Millie had set on his tray. "I appreciate the meal, but there was no need for all this fuss," he muttered. "Especially with you just arriving home this afternoon."

"All we did, after we heard what had happened, was move up the reservation with our driver by a couple of days," Elden responded. "Lancaster isn't far from here. Two hours."

"Like I said, he used you as an excuse to come home. We were staying with his uncle Elmer and aunt Dottie. The two of them snore like I've never heard in my life. We both slept with pillows over our heads, didn't we, Elden?" Millie beamed at him.

Elden smiled back. "We did."

"So…" Millie clapped her hands together. "I'm going to leave the rest of the stew in the refrigerator, the biscuits in the pie safe, and there's apple crisp on the counter and ice cream in your freezer. Now, I have to tell you the truth. I didn't make the stew, just the biscuits."

"So who *did* make it?" Tobit asked between mouthfuls. Once he was up and about, he wanted to be sure to seek her out and thank her. That thought surprised him. Wherever they lived, he and Charlie kept mostly to themselves, but there was something about this town that, for the first time in years, he wasn't already thinking about where they would try next.

"One of my sisters."

Millie had been a Koffman before she wed, so Tobit immediately thought of Cora Koffman.

*Cora made beef stew for him?* He found that hard to believe. The previous day when she'd offered to teach his classes, it had been obvious she still held it against him that he'd been given the permanent teaching position and she had not. She thought it was somehow his fault, which bothered him.

Usually he didn't worry much about what others thought about him. He and Elijah kept to themselves and encouraged others to do the same. But there was something about that pretty, petite young woman that made him feel things he didn't remember ever feeling before. Which made him wonder why he'd agreed to let the school board hire her in the first place.

"Our youngest sister, Jane, made the stew. She's becoming quite the cook," Millie answered over her shoulder as she headed for the kitchen. "She makes up her own recipes all the time and they're always delicious."

"I wouldn't say *always*. There was that time she put all that fresh basil in those muffins." Elden made a face. "I had to spit it out in my napkin."

"*Ya*, except for those muffins." Millie held up a finger as she left the parlor. "And maybe a few other things that weren't edible."

When his wife was gone, Elden turned back to Tobit. "Millie and I were talking on the way over, and if you like, I'd be happy to stay the night tonight. Stay as long as you like."

Tobit grimaced. "Why would you do that?" he asked, genuinely confused.

Elden approached the hospital bed Tobit was lying in. "In case you need something. Need help. You're bedridden," he added as if Tobit might have forgotten.

Tobit lowered his gaze, that sense of embarrassment creeping up again. "I have Elijah. We don't need any help. From anyone." Then afraid he had sounded rude, without making eye contact, he added, "But *danki* for the offer. Kind of you," he mumbled.

Elden stood beside the bed, arms crossed again, looking down at Tobit. "Where did you say you moved from?"

"Kansas." Tobit took another bite of biscuit.

"Well," Elden said slowly, "I don't know how they do things in Kansas, but here in Honeycomb…in Kent County, we support our friends, family and neighbors. Whatever you might need, we're here for you and we want to help."

Tobit kept his eyes on his food tray. "*Ya*, but we don't need any help, my boy and I."

Elden was quiet long enough that Tobit couldn't resist any longer and looked up. When he did, Elden met his gaze.

"You might not think you do, Tobit. But everyone

needs help occasionally." He slapped the bed with the palm of his hand. "So get used to it." He used his thumb to indicate the direction of the kitchen. "Now I'm going to gather that gorgeous wife of mine and take her home, but if you need something Elijah can't do for you, *anything*, you send him to fetch me. Or call my cell phone. It's only meant for emergencies, but I'll keep it on. I'll leave the number on your refrigerator. *Oll recht?*"

When Tobit realized Elden wasn't going to leave until he agreed, he nodded and mumbled, *"Oll recht."* And long after the two of them were gone, he was still wondering what *Gott* had in store for him here in Honeycomb.

## Chapter Three

Friday morning Cora stayed in bed longer than usual. She had woken up with a headache she suspected had been brought on by Tobit Lapp. But instead of going back to sleep, she'd lain awake in bed, trying to figure out what to do about the teaching position. She had wanted this so badly for so long. But if she did what Eleanor wanted and told the school board she wouldn't teach, would she have another opportunity?

It had been three days since Cora had learned of Tobit's injury and made her plea to the school board members to allow her to temporarily replace him. For three days, she'd been turning the dilemma over in her mind, weighing her options. A decision had to be made today because at nine thirty, Tobit was expecting her to come to his house to prepare for his classes. At nine thirty, she needed to be either at Tobit's, where she'd subject herself to his demands, or at Jim Mast's, resigning before she'd ever begun.

Time was running out, but she *still* didn't know what to do. She lay in bed a long time contemplating the matter and then, because she still didn't know what else to do, she decided to give the matter up to God. *Gott* would lead her to where she was meant to be.

Once she had completed her morning prayers, Cora prepared herself for the day and went downstairs. Breakfast had already been cleared away and the kitchen was quiet, for which she was thankful. It wasn't often in the Koffman household that she could find a moment alone. With so many sisters, all with their own opinions they had no trouble voicing, some days she felt as if she couldn't think for the din of her family.

After stoking the woodstove, Cora made herself some fresh coffee, and while it percolated, she prepared cinnamon sugar toast, one of her favorite breakfasts. It was something her mother made her when she was a child. Smiling at the memory, she sat down to enjoy her simple meal.

As she ate, she wondered where everyone was. The previous evening, the newlyweds, Beth and Jack, had joined them for supper. They had returned from their honeymoon and Beth was eager to spend time with their father. She had offered to have him over to her new apartment this morning to give Eleanor a chance to have time to herself, so he was likely there. Henry was building shelves in the storage room at the store. Jane and Willa were probably preparing to open the store for the day, and poor Millie, who was back earlier than expected, was on the way to her mother-in-law's doctor's appointment. Millie's husband, Elden, had offered to go with his mother. They lived on the same property in the big house where Elden had grown up and Lavinia was in the new *dawdi* house he'd built for her. However, Lavinia had insisted her new daughter-in-law escort her instead.

So, besides Charlie, who was still living with them, Eleanor was the only one unaccounted for. Cora hoped she'd gone to visit her friend Sara, who was expecting again and had been feeling poorly. Or maybe Eleanor was shopping without having to take their father. Their *dat* loved to shop and it was trying for whoever took him. He wanted to look at and buy everything. A few weeks previously, Cora and Willa had taken him to Spence's Bazaar and given him a few dollars to spend in the yard sale area. He'd purchased a tennis racket that had no strings, a tiny ceramic frog and a pair of women's red leather gloves. Which was better than the time he had bought a crate of live pigeons and wanted his daughters to prepare squab for dinner.

After breakfast, Cora tidied up and, seeing the time, forced herself to put on her cloak and black bonnet. She walked out of the house into the chilly morning and then hurried back inside to grab her canvas bag of teacher's supplies…just in case. Bag in hand, she went to the barn to hitch up a buggy. Over the summer, they had purchased a used buggy from a family in Rose Valley that was moving to Tennessee. Now they had two buggies and a wagon for the sisters to share. Hopefully, one would be available. If not, she'd take Jane's push-scooter.

In the barn, Cora discovered that all the horse-drawn vehicles were in their places and chose the smaller of the buggies. Unable to make up her mind about the job, she decided not to stop at the store and subject herself to any inquiries or opinions. She loved her family dearly, but no one knew how to mind their own business. And now that Elden, Jack and Charlie were members of the family, they were just as bad. Cora loved them as she would brothers, but she really didn't need any more advice.

Eyeing the store on their property as she guided their new driving horse, Bert, down the driveway, she was relieved to see that no one was outside to catch her slipping out. However, just as she thought she would make it safely to the road, Eleanor burst out the front door and hurried down the steps, waving at her while calling her name.

Cora sighed, veered at the split in their lane and entered the store's gravel parking lot.

"Headed to Jim Mast's, are you?" Eleanor asked, panting by the time she reached the buggy. She'd been in such a hurry to catch Cora that she hadn't taken the time to put on a coat.

Cora grimaced. She had considered driving off and pretending not to see Eleanor but feared that it would end badly. Eleanor might run down the lane after her or, worse yet, follow her.

As she waited for Eleanor to catch her breath and speak, Cora removed her prescription sunglasses from a case on the bench seat beside her. The morning air was crisp, but the sun was bright. She took her time removing her round wireframe glasses and put on the sunglasses. She placed the other glasses in the case for safekeeping.

"Telling the board you won't substitute for Tobit is the right thing to do, Cora," Eleanor encouraged. "Without a job that will take you away from home five days a week, you'll have time to concentrate on moving on with your life." She raised her hand. "Now don't say no straight off, but I was wondering if maybe we should contact the matchmaker in Seven Poplars."

Cora closed the eyeglass case with a loud snap, making it obvious without saying a word that she wasn't keen on the idea.

If Eleanor caught Cora's meaning, she ignored it. "But you like Sara Yoder."

"I do like her." Cora slipped on her calfskin driving gloves. "But I don't want anyone to find a husband for me." She looked down at her sister. "Because I don't want a husband."

"Oh, *nay*, don't say that." Eleanor patted Cora's knee. "*Mam* always said her greatest joy was marriage and her children."

"I didn't say I never want to marry. I'm not ready yet. But when I am, I'll do it on my own, *danki*." She leaned down. Eleanor was much taller than Cora, but the buggy seat sat high.

She disliked being the smallest of the sisters; it seemed as if she was never heard. "I have an idea, Ellie. Let's invite Sara Yoder over to talk about finding *you* a match." She smiled mischievously. She was tempted to tell her sister that she wondered if Eleanor's prosthetic was simply an excuse not to date. Cora suspected that Eleanor was as scared as the rest of them of the prospect of choosing the right husband. But Millie and Beth had found the perfect matches, so didn't that mean there were boys out there suitable for every Koffman sister?

But Cora kept her mouth shut because she didn't want to pick a fight with her big sister. Besides, if she didn't hurry she would be late to Tobit's. Or Jim Mast's. She still didn't know which direction she was headed.

Eleanor crossed her arms over her chest, shivering. "I should go in and rescue Jane and Millie from *Dat*. He's supposed to be helping bag up cookies Jane made this morning. He's eating more than he's bagging."

"I thought he was going to visit with Millie in her apartment."

Eleanor's nutmeg-brown eyes twinkled. "So did she."

The sisters met each other's gazes and smiled. No words were necessary. They both adored their father, even if he was a constant source of worry and occasional annoyance. But he had taken care of them during their childhoods; caring for him now was the least they could do for him.

"I'll see you when you get back," Eleanor said, walking away.

Cora took the reins more tightly in her hands and urged the driving horse forward. At the end of the driveway, she made a left and urged Bert into an easy trot. A mile down the road, she halted at the four-way stop and looked left, then right. Left would lead her to Jim Mast's. Right would take her to Tobit's.

She reached inside her cloak and pulled her watch from her dress pocket. It was nine twenty. She couldn't dally if she was going to Tobit's. Otherwise, she'd be late and that didn't seem like a smart way to begin her first real job. If she went left, she wouldn't be late because Jim wasn't expecting her, but if she wasn't taking the position, the sooner the board knew, the sooner they could make alternate plans.

She closed her eyes and groaned. She wanted so

badly to teach, but that didn't make sense, did it? Why would she voluntarily put herself in a situation where she would be forced to spend time with Tobit? A lot of time. Why would she go against Eleanor's wishes? Eleanor put others first, especially her immediate family. She always had Cora's best interest at heart when she asked Cora or even bossily directed Cora to do something.

And what if Eleanor was right? What if it was time for Cora to start seriously considering her future? She did want a husband and children, so why was she putting off trying to meet someone? While Cora preferred to stay home and read a book, Willa went to nearly every event held in Kent County meant to encourage young men and women of marriageable age to mingle and get to know each other with the goal of finding a spouse. Even Henry and now Jane went to such events. There was no reason why Cora couldn't go with them.

Still sitting at the stop sign, she looked right and then left and then right again. "What will it be, *Gott*?" she murmured. "I don't know what to do." She loosened the reins in her hands. "Take me where you want me to go."

Clutching the reins, her eyes closed, Cora repeated those words again and again. "Take me where you want me to go." And then when she didn't hear God's voice, when she didn't feel Him leading her in one direction or the other, she repeated them again, entreating Him to answer. And then she waited.

A pickup truck came up behind her, but instead of entering the crossroad and going left or right as she should have, she stubbornly waved him by.

And still *Gott* didn't tell her what to do.

Cora stared in the direction of the schoolhouse. She couldn't see it, but it was less than a mile away and Tobit's house was half a mile beyond it, on the far side of Raber's Feed Store.

She really wanted to teach school.

But now Tobit had ruined her opportunity by obstinately refusing to let her teach on her own. Gritting her teeth, Cora flipped the left-hand turn signal on the buggy, loosened the reins and headed for Jim Mast's.

Tobit checked the time again. He had been staring at the wind-up alarm clock on the table beside his hospital bed since he'd awoken that morning. Cora was supposed to be there any minute and he was nervous. But excited, too, and he didn't know which emotion worried him more. It wasn't like him to fancy a woman. He had closed off his heart to the silly notion of romantic love a long time ago. But there was something about Cora that set his mind drifting in directions he had no intention of going, not with Cora or anyone else.

She was different from other women he'd known. It had taken a great deal of nerve for her to walk into his house the other day and ask for the teaching job. She was a petite thing, but she stood tall with her shoulders back, and she made eye contact with the board members and the bishop. After it had been agreed that she would instruct Tobit's classes until he was well enough to teach again, they had discussed the details of her duties. She hadn't been afraid to ask questions or make suggestions, and he liked that about her.

Cora hadn't been afraid of him. Most women were. It was his size, he thought. There were few Amish men over six feet tall. He told himself that was what made them uncomfortable, although, over the years, more than one person had told him it was more his demeanor than his size. They suggested he should be nicer and smile more. He was never mean to anyone—and what if it wasn't in his nature to constantly smile?

Tobit glanced at the clock again. It was 9:31. She was late. Or maybe she wasn't coming. *Nay*, that couldn't be it. She was the one who asked for the job in the first place. If she wanted to be a teacher, this was the perfect opportunity to try her hand at it. Even from his bedside, he could help her learn to do the job effectively.

Another minute went by. "Elijah?" he called. "Did I hear a buggy in the yard?" When his son didn't answer, he shouted, "Elijah!"

The boy ran into the room, a dish towel in one hand, a bowl in the other. They'd had cold cereal and orange juice for breakfast. No coffee. Tobit hadn't had coffee since his accident because his son didn't know how to make it. Earlier in the week, Tobit had been in too much pain to try to explain the steps to him. That, coupled with his stomach upset by the medications he'd been prescribed. Now he felt like he needed a cup. He had a headache and he was…nervous. Nothing made him nervous. It had to be because he was in caffeine withdrawal. That was a real thing. He'd read about it in a magazine once in a dentist's office.

"Are you *oll recht, Dat*?"

"I'm fine. Is my teaching assistant here? I thought I heard a buggy."

"Nobody's here, *Dat*."

Elijah would be thirteen come Christmas and suddenly he was beginning to look more like a man than a child. Had Tobit been the kind of person to dwell on his feelings, the idea of his little boy growing into a man might have worried him. Tobit did the best he could, but raising a child alone felt like stumbling in the dark while tripping over stools and constantly righting them.

"She's not coming. I should have known this wasn't going to work out," he grumbled. Tobit smoothed the bedding across his lap. Earlier in the morning, he had trimmed his beard and had his son fetch him a clean shirt. He didn't know why he worried what Cora thought of him.

Tobit looked at his son. Elijah was still standing in the doorway, looking like he wanted to say something. "What?"

The boy hesitated. "I was just thinking that I hope she does come," he said in a small voice. "Charlie says she's really nice."

"Oh, Charlie says, does he?" Charlie was in sixth grade with Elijah and one of his problem children. The boy wasn't bad, but he couldn't sit still and didn't have the attention God gave a fly. And he was a terrible student. Tobit frowned. "What's his relationship to Cora Koffman again?"

Elijah wiped the water off the cereal bowl with the dish towel. "Cora's sister married Jack Lehman. Charlie is Jack's brother. Charlie lives with his brother... Well, I think he lives in the big house with Cora and the other Koffmans now."

"So the big Koffman girl is married to Jack Lehman."

Elijah shook his head. "Beth's married to Jack. Millie

married Elden Yoder. They live across the street from the Koffmans on Plum Road."

Tobit glanced at the clock again. Cora was now six minutes late. What kind of teacher couldn't make an appointment on time? He frowned and returned his attention to his son. "I wasn't aware Charlie didn't live with his parents. Why does Charlie live with his brother?" He shook his head. "Why's he with the Koffmans?"

"I don't know why. I think his brother Jack takes care of him, but Jack and Beth live in an apartment above the Koffman store. Charlie stayed with the Koffmans when Beth and Jack were in Pennsylvania after their wedding. Charlie was supposed to move into the apartment when his brother got back." He shrugged. "I don't know why he didn't."

Tobit looked at the clock again. It was nine forty-five. Cora wasn't coming. The school board would have to come up with another solution. There was nothing he could do about it, except prepare lesson plans for whomever they hired. Surely someone in the community would step up and offer to be the substitute, someone who didn't want to be a teacher but was willing to do it because it was needed. Cora had been a poor choice on the part of the school board. He should never have agreed to it. It was better this way, he told himself.

The question was, why was he so disappointed?

# Chapter Four

"*Dat?*"

Tobit felt a tap on his shoulder.

"*Dat?*"

Elijah's voice. Tentative.

Tobit groaned. He hadn't meant to fall asleep. When he'd realized Cora wasn't coming and she wouldn't be substituting for him, he'd had Elijah bring him his school satchel. No matter who temporarily took over for him, papers had to be graded, and plans for each of his classes in the one-room schoolhouse had to be made. He'd only closed his eyes for a moment while grading a stack of spelling tests. The third graders in Honeycomb were terrible spellers, and the pain of that knowledge, coupled with the pain from his leg that radiated through his body, had made him sleepy.

"*Dat*," Elijah repeated.

"Maybe you should let him sleep." A feminine voice.

For a dreamy moment, Tobit thought it was his wife, Aida. But of course, it wasn't. It couldn't be. Which led him to wonder who—

He opened his eyes suddenly, jerking when he did. His clipboard with the attached spelling tests clattered off the side of the bed and onto the floor. His gaze settled on a pretty face and he cleared his throat. "Cora."

"Should I come back?" she asked, peering down at him.

Cora was as cute as a button in a green tab dress and starched white prayer *kapp*. Her wireframe glasses made her dark brown eyes look bigger and brighter. She was an attractive young woman, there was no denying that, and he wondered how old she was. Early to midtwenties? The reddish-blond hair that framed her face was a color that prompted the urge to feel it between his fingers.

"You're late," Tobit blurted, his words sounding gruffer than he intended.

"I apologize."

She pressed her rosy lips together, giving no explanation for her tardiness, which annoyed him. At the same time, he admired her grit. Though people always felt like they had to provide an explanation with an apology, it wasn't always necessary.

He pushed himself farther upright in the bed, more uncomfortable receiving her this way than he had been earlier in the week. Maybe the excruciating pain he'd been suffering the day she'd come to ask for the job had dulled his sensibilities. Bed rest was for the old, the infirm and sometimes for women with pregnancy complications, not for able-bodied men like himself. He found it embarrassing.

"I thought you'd changed your mind."

She met his gaze. "I did not." She stood under his

scrutiny without fidgeting, a canvas tote in her hand. "I'll make a good teacher." She set down her bag and began to pick up the spelling tests off the hardwood floor.

"It's not as easy as you might think," he warned. "First to eighth graders all squeezed into a single room that's too small. Students at all different levels are either clambering for your attention or hoping you don't see what mischief they're getting into."

"No need to worry," she answered with tenacity. "I'll make out just fine."

He narrowed his gaze, watching her closely. "And what do your mother and father think about you working? Most women your age are married with a *boppli* on her hip or are betrothed, and busy looking for a husband."

"I'm not looking for a husband." She stood up, tests in both hands, and squared her shoulders. "And our *mam* passed two years ago. *Dat*—" she broke eye contact "—he supports our endeavors."

*Endeavors,* Tobit thought. Good word and used well. He wondered how she knew it. When he'd left his last job in Indiana, he'd been warned that when it came to schooling in Delaware, the Old Order communities lagged behind others. According to a school board member who had tried to convince him to stay, many children in Delaware weren't remaining in school beyond the sixth grade. Following the beliefs of previous generations, many elders believed that no education was needed beyond learning to read, write and do simple math. He wondered if Cora had remained in school through the eighth grade, or beyond, or if she was self-taught.

"Jim Mast told me Honeycomb hasn't had a woman teacher," he said, accepting a stack of the test papers from her. The one on the very top, Jerimiah Mast's, had the first two words so poorly spelled that he wanted to toss it back on the floor. Of course, he would never do such a thing. Students like Jerimiah deserved as much of his attention as his twin sister, who he suspected would have gotten every word correct.

Cora handed Tobit the rest of the tests and leaned down to pick up the last couple. "Shall we start with these?" she asked. "While we grade them, you can tell me what I'll need to know for Monday. I see you use a red pen. I brought one with me."

Tobit began dividing the tests by class as the fourth- and fifth-grade tests had gone down with the others. "Elijah, pull that chair up for Cora," he instructed, nodding toward the kitchen chair they were using for guests.

Not many folks had visited, which was fine with Tobit. He preferred that he and Elijah stay on the fringe of a community. They attended church, of course, but they rarely participated in visiting Sundays and they never had anyone over for supper. Cora's uncle Bishop Cyrus had come every day since the accident. There was some leeway in Honeycomb regarding what church district folks belonged to. Often folks joined according to proximity or family relationships, but in each place they had lived, Tobit joined whichever district he thought would be most likely to leave him and Elijah to themselves. So far, he hadn't chosen one here in Honeycomb, but Bishop Cyrus was pushing hard for his district.

Elijah carried the chair to the bedside. "Need anything else, *Dat*?" he asked.

"I don't think so. You can go ahead and start on the horse stall. It won't clean itself."

"*Ya, Dat*. And then I can take my pony cart out?"

"You may. But stay on the property. I don't want you on the road with me laid up in bed."

Cora took the seat, as Elijah hurried out of the room. "You're raising a nice boy there. He seems to be very attentive to you."

Never having been one to know what to do with a compliment, Tobit muttered *"Danki"* under his breath. He handed her the third-grade spelling tests that hadn't been checked yet. "Correct the misspellings and put the grade at the top with a circle around it, and then when you finish a class," he instructed, "you put the score in the grade book." He picked up the black book from his bedside table and waved it at her.

She pulled her red pen out of her bag and made an event of clicking the top. "And then they retest next week on the words they missed plus some new ones?"

He looked up from the test on top of the fifth-graders' pile. "What?" He frowned. "*Nay*. Next week there's a new list of words."

She hesitated before she said, "Then how do they learn the correct spelling?"

He scratched a line through the misspelled word that was supposed to be "barefoot" but was spelled "bear fut" and looked up. "There's a list of words for each grade they need to get through in a year. How will we get through the list if students repeatedly have the same words?"

She looked at him quizzically. "I assume the words get increasingly more difficult as the year progresses. Shouldn't they learn the easier words first?"

He exhaled in frustration. She'd been here five minutes and was already telling him how he should run his school. "It's how spelling tests are given, Cora. You'd know that if you'd taught before. It was the same when I was in school and I suspect for you, too."

"*Ya*, but that doesn't mean it's the best way to—"

"And how would that work, anyway?" he interrupted. "How many hours would I...*you* spend a week writing individual spelling tests for every student in the school? We have forty-three children in eight grades. How would you even give the tests?" he demanded.

"I would think the students could—"

He cut her off again. *"Nay."* He returned his attention to the paper he was grading. "Let's get these done, and then I'll show you what's planned for next week. We'll break it down by class." He didn't look at her. "I have been making notes on each student so you know what you're dealing with."

"I know every girl and boy who goes to this school," she said curtly.

"*Okey.* So you know I have a girl with Downs."

"Of course. Apple Detweiler. Everyone in Honeycomb knows Apple has Down syndrome."

"Fine," he muttered. "But do you know that Emma—" he held up her spelling test "—who is in the fifth grade still inverts letters and numbers? Or that her twin sister, Sarah—" he pulled the girl's test from the stack "—doesn't have a learning issue but copies her sister's work if I don't separate them?"

Cora met his gaze without flinching. "I did not, but now I do." She didn't look away.

"Are you always this grumpy with everyone?"

Her question took him by such surprise, but before he could respond, she continued.

*"Nay."* She drew out the word. "That's not quite the right question." She waggled her red pen at him. "I already know that you're grumpy with your son—"

"I'm not—"

"And your students." She spoke over him. "With the school board, with my uncle the bishop and me, of course, so… I guess my question is, is there anyone you're *not* grumpy with?"

Tobit was so taken aback by her words that he just sat and stared at her. Then as much to his surprise as hers, he laughed. He had no idea why. Maybe because she had gotten the better of him and folks didn't usually do that.

She flashed him a smile and went back to grading papers, and he thought that maybe having Cora Koffman teach for him wasn't going to be so bad after all.

Cora pulled the schoolhouse door shut, checked to be sure it had locked and sighed with relief as she went down the steps. It was only three thirty in the afternoon, but she felt she had been there for days.

"I'll bring the buggy around," Charlie offered. "I already hitched up. We're stopping at Elijah's, right?"

She sighed again, not sure she had the energy to face Tobit right now. She knew he would grill her about how the day had gone, and she'd have to relay every misstep she'd made. And there had been many. But they had agreed they would meet so she had to go. *"Ya,"* she answered, slowly coming down the steps that led from the cloakroom.

"Yes!" Charlie pumped his fist. "I told Elijah I'd help him throw straw down from the barn loft. It's going to get cold tonight and he wants to make sure the animals have warm bedding."

*"Ya*, we'll stop, but we're not staying long," she warned. Right now, all she wanted to do was go home, crawl under the covers in her bed and figure out how to get out of this mess she'd made for herself.

Cora hadn't been foolish enough to think everything would go perfectly on her first day. She was aware that she was new to teaching and even if the students knew her from the community, she would be a change from Tobit. She understood that she would have to learn how to manage her time and her students', but everything that could have gone wrong had.

Her first day as a teacher had begun with her struggling to start a fire in the old woodstove in the rear of the classroom. She'd been building fires since she was six, when her father had taught her the proper technique. But it had rained the night before and there had been no kindling in the cloakroom so she'd had to use some from the outside. Charlie ended up getting the fire going for her, but not before she'd filled the room with smoke and they'd had to open all the windows, making it even colder.

And the day hadn't gotten any better. She'd kept confusing the twin Byler boys, even though she knew full well that Jon had the small birthmark on his cheek and Jacob didn't, and they'd pointed it out loud every time she did it. She misread Tobit's detailed instructions and gave her three seventh graders the same assignment they'd completed two weeks before. She reread the same page twice while reading to her first graders and they'd let her, only to point out her error *after* she'd done it. She'd made a mistake on a simple math problem on the board with the fourth graders, bumped into a student's desk, knocking his books to the floor, and lost two sixth-grade boys. And that had all been before noon when she discovered she'd forgotten the nice lunch she'd packed for herself and had to share a mushy peanut butter sandwich with Charlie. And she disliked peanut butter.

"Bye, Teacher!" one of her first graders called as the child headed down the driveway with a group of girls on push scooters. Each of them wore a fluorescent yellow or green vest over their jacket.

"See you tomorrow, Anna." Cora waved. "And don't forget your scarf. It's going to be chilly."

As the girls pushed their scooters toward the road, a female voice called from behind. "Cora! There you are. So glad I didn't miss you."

Cora turned to see Ruby Detweiler walking out of the woods behind the schoolhouse. There was a path that led to Mulberry Road, which ran parallel to Clover, where the school was located. Five of the Jonathan Detweiler children attended the school. Three Detweiler children had aged out of school and three more would eventually attend. And from the look of Ruby this morning, Cora could safely assume that another was on the way.

"Ruby." Cora smiled even though she didn't feel

much like it. "Did one of your children forget something?"

Ruby huffed and puffed her way toward Cora. "Only the note I've been trying to send to Tobit. He ignored my first one. I thought maybe I might have a better chance talking with you."

"Is there a problem with one of your little ones?" Cora met her in the middle of the driveway. Ruby Detweiler was a sturdy woman of around forty who seemed to have endless energy, which was a good thing, with eleven children and another on the way.

"*Ya*, Minnie and Apple are driving me to distraction wanting to know when rehearsal will begin for the Christmas program."

All of Ruby's children went by nicknames, which annoyed some of the members of their community because they had to remember both names. Minnie was actually Anna, but Cora couldn't remember Apple's. The third grader drew a picture of an apple on her papers, a surprisingly good drawing for her age and the fact that she had Down syndrome.

"The annual Christmas program," Cora repeated. She was so tired that she could barely think.

Was there still a Christmas program at school? Although it had been many years since she and her sisters had attended the Clover school, as they had called it, they had continued to attend the Christmas program. But they hadn't gone since their mother's death. Their mother had loved the Christmas presentations at the little school in Honeycomb and often enjoyed several per season, always dragging at least one of her daughters with her. After she passed, they all had wished they had gone more often with her.

"It's November and the girls say they haven't heard a word about it," Ruby said. "They said that when they asked their teacher, he said he didn't know anything about a Christmas program, and you know how he can be." She tightened her woolen scarf at the knot beneath her chin. "He's not one for discussion."

Cora had to suppress a smile. "I don't know anything about plans for the program. You know this was my first day, but I'll be sure to speak to Tobit about it."

"It's so good of you to substitute for Tobit." Ruby lowered her voice as if fearing someone might hear her, although there was no one left in the schoolyard but the two of them and Charlie. "I was praying you were the one they'd hire. A woman. My husband told me to mind my own knitting, but I talked to every one of our school board members and told them it was time we hired a woman. I didn't care if Wheatey agreed or not. Seven Poplars has had women teaching at their schools for years. Hickory Grove, too."

"I thank you for that," Cora said as Charlie approached, the sound of the horse's hooves on the gravel making it hard to hear. "Let me see what I can find out about the Christmas program."

"You think we should have one, don't you?" Ruby asked. "You know Christmas isn't Christmas in Honeycomb unless the children get to sing carols and recite from the Bible. And then, of course, there's the cookies and hot chocolate afterward with friends and neighbors."

Cora glanced at Charlie, who looked eager to be on

his way. It seemed as if he and Elijah were becoming good friends. "Would you like a ride home, Ruby?"

"*Ach*, goodness no. It's two miles in a buggy around to my place. I'll cut right through the woods like the children." She wrinkled her freckled nose, giving the impression of being younger than her years. "Gives me a chance to hear myself think. I'd like to tell you I spend it in prayer, but the truth is, I mostly let my mind wander and don't think about supper or the dirty clothes piled high in the laundry."

Cora waved goodbye to Ruby, passed her book satchel up to Charlie and stepped into the buggy. Fifteen minutes later, she stood in the doorway between Tobit's hallway and the parlor. She'd half hoped he'd be asleep, and she could go home and have a hot bath before dinner, but he was awake. And it appeared he'd been waiting for her. He was wearing a clean shirt and had combed his curly hair.

"Run late today?" Tobit greeted, glancing at the wind-up alarm clock beside his bed. He looked a little better today than he had on Friday. He had more color in his face, and it wasn't so strained. She suspected he'd been in pain the previous times she'd been here, although he hadn't mentioned it.

Cora took a deep breath and walked into the parlor as if she'd been looking forward to the visit rather than dreading it. "*Nay*. Certainly not. I dismissed at three fifteen and two of the Mast girls stayed to help me tidy up."

"They swept the whole classroom?"

She nodded. "And the cloakroom. I'd forgotten how big it is. I had some of the older girls take the little girls who don't know their letters yet out there and they read to them instead of doing it myself."

"You let them drag desks into the cloakroom?" he asked, disapprovingly.

She paused before speaking because while lying in bed the night before trying to figure out how to deal with him, she realized that there was no need for her to respond to his grumpiness in kind. Her mother had always said that treating all people with kindness and grace was important because you never knew what was going on in someone's private life.

"I did not let them take their desks to the cloakroom." She eyed him using her *teacher's* voice, which was enunciated and authoritative. "They sat in a circle on the floor. It worked out quite well," she told him, glad she had thought to start with a success before giving him the opportunity to gloat over her failures. "It worked so well—" she dropped her satchel on the chair beside his bed "—that I think that tomorrow I'll bring an old rag rug from home and we're going to call it the reading rug. I think even the boys will enjoy having a special place for reading, and it cuts back on the noise in the classroom." While separating the boys from girls wasn't required, Cora had learned quickly that it worked out much better for certain activities.

He drew his mouth so tightly that his lips were pursed. *"Reading rug."*

*"Ya."* She began to pull the student papers she'd collected out of her bag and set them on the nightstand beside his bed.

"Hmm."

As she waited for him to tell her why it was a terrible

idea and she wasn't to do it again, she dug for her pen in her satchel. Cora had no intention of grading papers with Tobit this afternoon. She was too tired, and her feet hurt because she'd been foolish enough to wear new shoes on her first of school, a mistake she hadn't made since she was in the third grade. She'd grade papers after supper when the family gathered in their parlor to read, stitch or play checkers with their father.

"I can see how that might work," Tobit mused aloud.

Surprised by his reaction, she looked up, speechless.

"It's a good idea," he continued. "I had something like that in the last school where I taught but we had two classrooms, one that opened into the other, so I had the space. It hadn't occurred to me to try the cloakroom." He nodded. "Very resourceful, Cora." He picked up the pile of student papers. "Let's see what we have here."

Finding her pen, she grabbed a notepad. "Before I forget, Ruby Detweiler stopped by. She wanted to know what the plans were for the Christmas program."

He didn't look up from the essay Anna May Byler had written. "What Christmas program?"

"The children in Honeycomb do it every year. You know, they show their families what they've been doing in class, sing, and recite. We have cookies and hot chocolate afterward. Like an end-of-the-year program only for Christmas."

"I don't do Christmas programs." He drew a line through something Anna May had written. "Did Johnny and Noah sneak off?"

She'd gone to the edge of the woods to call for the two sixth graders. Only when she'd threatened to get their parents had they reluctantly come out of hiding and returned to the schoolhouse. "How did you know?" she asked in a small voice.

He still didn't look up from the paper he was grading. "They did it my first day, too."

Cora had a terrible urge to giggle at the thought of this big, burly man being played by sixth-grade boys. But that seemed unprofessional, so she bit down on her lower lip. "I made them split wood during recess as punishment."

"Good choice. I had them pull weeds. They were just testing you," he told her. "They won't do it again." He circled a grade on the top of Anna May's paper. "You don't look as frazzled as I expected. Tell me how the day went."

So Cora did. She relayed the few positives she could recall and all the mistakes she'd made. He agreed with the missteps, but she was pleasantly surprised that he refrained from being critical. Together they adjusted the curriculum for the next couple of days and agreed to meet again on Wednesday. Because Tobit was teaching Elijah at home for now so the boy would be there to help his father, Cora agreed to grade his work for Tobit. Tobit said Elijah would take criticism better from her.

In less than an hour, they'd discussed several topics and Cora packed her book satchel to leave. "Charlie and I best get going. My sister Eleanor hates it when we're late for supper."

Tobit watched her prepare to go. "What are you having for supper?"

The question didn't seem odd to her. Folks in Honeycomb loved their food and talked about it constantly: what they were baking, what they were having for supper, what new recipes they'd found in the latest edition of *The Budget*, an international Amish-Mennonite newspaper. "Hmm. Let's see. I think Jane, my youngest sister, said spaghetti and meatballs. And garlic bread."

Tobit raised a dark eyebrow. "Spaghetti and meatballs? No *hasenpfeffer*? Not very Amish."

She laughed. "I don't like rabbit."

"We're having scrambled eggs and toast again, so *hasenpfeffer* sounds pretty good."

He shrugged when she looked at him in response to the meager supper. "It's something Elijah can make. The eggs are usually a little runny and the toast is burnt, but it's enough to satisfy the body. If not the soul," he added.

She nodded in understanding. The boy was doing his best for his father. What more could one ask of a twelve-year-old?

"I'll see you Wednesday after school," she told Tobit as she turned to go.

"See you Wednesday. And Cora?"

*"Ya?"* She glanced at him over her shoulder.

"Don't worry. It gets easier."

His comment touched Cora, and as she walked out of his house, she was surprised to find herself smiling. He had been so kind and supportive when she'd relayed all the mistakes she'd made that she was finding it hard to hold on to the fact that he had gotten the job and she hadn't.

*Nay*, it was worse than that.

She feared she liked him.

## Chapter Five

Tobit eased down to sit on the edge of the hospital bed and catch his breath. He was shocked that after two weeks of bed rest, he was winded by walking across the room with his crutches. He and Elden had just returned home after a doctor's appointment and X-rays, and then they'd had their driver stop for groceries. When Elden had offered to go with him to the appointment, Tobit had tried to convince him that he didn't need an escort. However, by the time Tobit had reached the Mennonite driver's minivan that morning, he'd been glad to have the assistance.

Because he'd known he'd be gone a good part of the day, Tobit had sent Elijah to school that morning. He'd feared the boy would resist, but Elijah had been surprisingly open to the idea of attending, saying he missed his new friends, particularly Charlie Lehman. Tobit thought it would be good for his son to spend the day with his classmates. And Elijah could give him a report on how Cora was doing in her second week of teaching, although he didn't ask his son to spy for him.

He figured he would ask his son some general questions about how things were progressing over supper.

It was Elijah who'd suggested that his father buy groceries while he was in town. Several folks in Honeycomb had offered to prepare food or shop for him, but he'd repeatedly insisted they were fine. That wasn't a lie. Although his refrigerator and cupboards were close to bare, there was still plenty of eggs and milk. Truthfully, Tobit wasn't sure he could face another night of scrambled eggs with hot sauce, especially when there wasn't any bread left. The previous night, they'd eaten a toasted, stale hot dog roll with butter to go with their eggs.

Tobit had intended to do his own shopping for groceries, but he'd never made it into the store after his appointments. Elden had shopped for him because while the doctor had given Tobit permission to get up for short periods, he was still technically on bed rest. Even if Tobit *had* been allowed to go into the store using his crutches, he'd been so exhausted from the doctor's visit that he wasn't sure he could have managed.

Tobit looked up at Elden. "Thank you for grocery shopping for me."

Elden had insisted on changing the sheets on the hospital bed and was busy bundling them up to put them in the laundry room for Elijah to wash later.

"I feel bad that you've given up a whole day," Tobit continued. "I know you have better things to do than play nursemaid to me."

Elden frowned. "I told you this is the sort of thing we do for each other in Honeycomb. Besides, you're my friend." He shrugged, hugging the dirty sheets to his chest. "There isn't anything I wouldn't do for you. And I think you'd do the same for me if I were in your place. I'll be right back."

While Elden was gone, Tobit mulled over what Elden had said and couldn't help but smile. He couldn't remember the last time someone had called him a friend. He wasn't sure anyone had *ever* said it, at least not since he'd been a schoolboy. But while it felt good to hear the word *friend*, Tobit wasn't comfortable with such talk. His aunt and uncle who'd raised him had discouraged speaking about feelings in their household. Tobit had always had a roof over his head and food in his belly, but it was lonely for him growing up in the joyless place. His uncle was a fire-and-brimstone man with strict rules and punishment for disobeying them. Tobit had been expected to work hard and keep his mouth shut like his cousins, which was especially true regarding personal feelings.

Elden walked back into the parlor. "I threw the sheets in the washer. When Elijah gets home, he can put them in the dryer."

Tobit wiped the perspiration off his brow. Even though it was cool outside, the short walk into the house had left him overheated. "You didn't have to do that."

"Nope, I didn't. But it didn't take any effort to drop them into the washer." Elden stroked his beard, which was short enough for him to be recognized as a new husband to other Amish. "Tell me again what you were doing up on the windmill."

"Trying to fix one of the blades that wobbled a bit. It was a simple enough matter to right. I still don't know exactly what happened. One second I was standing on the ledge, the next, I was lying on the ground with Elijah standing over me." He exhaled trying not to think about all the ways it could have been worse. He could have died in the fall. What would have become of his son, then? He cleared his throat, pushing the fear back. "But thankfully, I'm going to be fine. By the new year, I'll be as good as new."

*"Ya,"* Elden agreed. "Sounded like the doctor had nothing but good news on your leg."

"He said he'd check the X-ray results, but he's happy with my progress. Said most folks weren't off pain pills so soon after an injury like mine." Tobit shook his head as he slid farther onto the bed to elevate his leg. "But I didn't like how they made me feel. Now I'm just taking something over-the-counter when I need it."

"All good news." Elden shrugged. "And you got out of the house for a few hours and Elijah got to go to school. You think you'll send him back now that you're allowed to get out of bed if you need to? Cora said she hoped that once you could take care of yourself during the day, you'd let him go. She figured he could come home during lunch to check on you and see if you need anything."

"Cora says, does she?" Tobit asked before he had enough sense to keep his mouth shut.

After spending a good part of the day with Elden, it was obvious that he thought a great deal of the Koffman family, and that included Cora. In fact, his friend had spent a good deal of time extolling the young woman's virtues. He'd talked about what a good student she had been and how she'd continued her education at home under her mother's tutelage, something not heard of often in Kent County, Delaware. In the winter months, Elden said that Cora still checked out library books to read and that she often wrote articles for *The Budget*.

That explained where her excellent vocabulary came from. Tobit had self-taught himself, and he'd found that the best way to do that was to read. The kind of reading material permitted varied from church to church, depending on where he and Elijah had lived. He'd kept to himself so much, though, that no one ever knew what he read.

Elden came to the bedside, turned the chair around so that the backrest faced the bed and straddled it. He gave a long whistle. "Pretty girl, that Cora."

Tobit stretched out on the mattress and slowly lifted his leg to prop it up on the pillows Elden placed for that purpose. "*Ya*, she's pretty, all right." He closed his eyes, feeling a headache coming on.

It wasn't the first time since Cora had come into his life. She'd stopped by every other day since she began substituting, and he often had a headache after she left. He wasn't sleeping well, either. Every time he closed his eyes, he saw her in his head. Then, against his will, he found himself going over every word they had exchanged that afternoon, chastising himself for anything he had said that he wished he hadn't and then all the things he should have said.

To his immense relief, Cora was doing well. Each day she had more positive outcomes to report and fewer missteps. While they didn't agree on everything, she seemed open-minded to his advice and tried his suggestions. He was beginning to see that she had some good ideas, although he was hesitant to encourage her to veer from his instructions. He wasn't sure why.

"Want a piece?" Elden asked, extracting a pack of peppermint gum from his pocket.

Tobit hesitated. He didn't chew gum often, but he worried his breath was bad. He should have thought to brush his teeth when he was in the bathroom, but it was too late now. He'd been on his crutches too long already and his leg throbbed. *"Danki,"* he said, accepting the gum.

The men unwrapped their confections, popped them into their mouths and chewed. As he balled up the wrapper to drop into the trash can beside his bed, Tobit noted some dust on the nightstand. He'd ask Elijah to run a rag over it as soon as he got home. He didn't want Cora to think he couldn't keep his house clean. Ordinarily, it was as spotless as any Amish home he'd visited, but a twelve-year-old boy couldn't be expected to keep a house as well as a grown woman. Or man.

Elden chewed his gum. "She's single, you know," he said, speaking slowly, as if the thought had just crossed his mind.

Tobit doubted it.

"Koffman girls make fine wives, I can tell you that firsthand," Elden continued. "Millie has made me one of the happiest men in Honeycomb. I'd say the happiest, but my brother-in-law Jack would disagree because he feels the same way about his Beth."

Tobit closed his eyes and chewed the gum, enjoying the cool peppermint taste.

"You ought to marry her before another man sweeps her up."

Tobit's eyes flew open as he almost choked on his gum. "Marry her? Me?" He coughed and sat up.

Elden shrugged. "Why not? She's smart and pretty and I have an idea she could deal with you when you get cantankerous."

"I don't get *cantankerous*." Tobit knew that he did, but he was trying to deflect. "You're a strange lot in Honeycomb."

Elden grinned. "How so?"

"For one, you spend a good deal of time discussing what other folks ought to do. Marry Cora." He snorted, still not believing Elden had made the outrageous suggestion. "And another thing, you've got a vocabulary beyond any Amish I know, even in less strict communities."

"Cora," Elden said.

Tobit frowned. "Cora what?"

"She throws around big words. Sometimes we pick them up."

Tobit's mouth twitched at the pun, which he couldn't tell if it had been intended or not. But he didn't smile. "I am not marrying Cora. I'm not marrying anyone," he added quickly.

Elden rested his forearms on the chairback and leaned forward, growing serious. "I can't imagine what it must have been like for you, losing your wife. I've barely been married a month and I can't begin to think what my life would be without my Millie. She doesn't just make me happy. She makes me—" he hesitated "—she makes me a better man. She makes me a better son, and a better servant of God." He studied Tobit while Tobit said nothing. "How long ago did you say since your wife passed? Nine years?"

"Going on ten." Tobit did not make eye contact. He didn't want to be rude, especially after Elden had been so kind today, but he wanted out of this conversation even more than the one about Cora. It was these kinds of conversations, this one in particular, that made him want to move often. That caused him to keep to himself wherever he lived. Because it was the only way he could keep up the deception that he was a widowed man.

Elden kept talking. "I imagine the hurt never goes away, but you know our faith tells us that God calls us to be a husband. A father, if we're so blessed. He who finds a wife finds a good thing and obtains favor from the Lord. Here in Honeycomb, we encourage our widows and widowers to remarry after a year of mourning."

"I won't marry again," Tobit said, staring at a space on the wall across from him.

"But what if God has another plan?" Elden hesitated, but when Tobit didn't respond, he went on. "Did you know that Cora had decided not to take the job substituting for you?"

"What?" Tobit whipped around to look at his friend.

Elden leaned forward to rest his chin on his folded arms. "Now, it might be smart for you to keep this to yourself, but Millie told me that the Friday before she started teaching, she drove to Jim Mast's to tell him she changed her mind. Got all the way to his driveway but couldn't do it. Something made her turn her buggy around and come here instead."

Tobit was so surprised by this revelation that he didn't know what to say. Cora had never said a word about it.

"Millie believes it was God who made her turn

around. She thinks she was meant to have this job. That you two were meant to work together."

As Tobit tried to figure out the best way to respond, Elijah, bless him, burst through the back door.

"*Dat*, we're home," the boy called from the kitchen. "Charlie and Cora are with me!"

His son must have let their dog in because a moment later, their black-and-white border collie burst into the parlor and raced around the round rag rug in front of the sofa.

"Boots," Elijah called. "Get out of there! You know you're not supposed to be in the parlor." He came to the doorway and clapped his hands together, leaning down to get the dog's attention. "Come on, girl. Good girl," he said when the dog reached the bed and whipped around to race in the opposite direction. "Hey ya, Elden," he said as he left the room with the border collie on his heels.

"Hey," Elden called after him. Then he turned to Tobit, who had slid up in the bed until he was sitting fully upright. "You need any help to do anything before I go?"

Tobit shook his head. "*Nay*, you've already done too much."

"We could argue on that subject for the next hour, but I'll say goodbye. If you need me, though—" he pointed "—you know to—"

"Call you," Tobit interrupted.

Cora walked through the doorway, her book satchel in hand. "Afternoon, Elden." She smiled at him. Then she turned to Tobit and greeted him, still smiling, but her face was softer when she spoke to him. Hesitant, perhaps. "Tobit."

"Cora," Tobit replied stiffly, a bit surprised by how happy he was that she had decided to stop by. He'd thought she wouldn't since she'd been there the day before and stayed nearly until suppertime.

"Be seeing you soon," Elden told Tobit. With a grin, he winked at him and walked out of the room.

"What was that all about?" Cora asked, watching her brother-in-law take his leave.

"What was what about?" Tobit shifted on the bed, suddenly looking uncomfortable.

"Elden winked at you. Like you two had an inside joke going on." She narrowed her gaze suspiciously. "You weren't talking about me, were you?"

Tobit made a face, insinuating her observation was ridiculous, which made her warier.

"Why would we be talking about you?" he asked, trying to look innocent. Which wasn't convincing.

"I don't know," she said slowly, wondering what they had been talking about if it wasn't her. She'd have to corner Elden and quiz him later.

"How was your day?" Tobit asked, obviously trying to change the conversation.

She was tempted to push him on the matter but decided against it. She didn't want to argue with Tobit today. Or any day, truthfully, because the better she got to know him, the more she liked him. Cora wasn't sure what to do with that feeling, especially because she sensed that although they may have gotten off on the wrong foot, he seemed to like her as well. "You first. How was your appointment?"

Tobit relayed what the doctor had said, and she was

immensely relieved to hear that he was on the mend. She'd been awake half the night worrying about him. The other half of the night she spent contemplating how she felt about what she'd begun to realize was her attraction to him. How could she have a romantic interest in a man who had stolen her job? A man who hadn't been all that friendly to her at first. And he was a widower eight years older than her with a child. Never once when she had thought about the man she might marry someday had she considered one much older than her. She had never contemplated being a stepmother, either. The idea of it scared her. Being the mother of a newborn was daunting enough, but a boy Elijah's age needed someone with experience in such matters, didn't he?

These thoughts had kept her awake until dawn had streaked the sky. Only then did she realize it was foolish to allow her worries to cause her lack of sleep. While she might suspect Tobit was attracted to her, it was more than likely he was getting used to their arrangement. Only a foolish schoolgirl would let her mind play tricks on her. She was too pragmatic for such nonsense. And too busy.

Cora crossed her arms. "I'm glad you're on the mend. It must have been a relief to hear the doctor say so. Did he say how long you have to stay off your leg?"

Tobit wore what looked like a new shirt, and the hue made his eyes look even bluer. He had trimmed his beard so that it was closely cropped to his jaw, which gave her a better look at the shape of his face. It was funny how quickly she'd gotten used to his bearish appearance. Now, he looked handsome to her.

"Out of bed in another week or so, but I'll have to

use the crutches." He indicated the wooden set leaning against the wall. "Then I'll have to be very careful. Light housework, no barn work."

"And no windmill repair," she suggested, her tone teasing.

He flashed a smile that gave her butterflies and she smiled back. He'd never looked at her that way before and it made her feel uncertain but lighthearted at the same time.

"The doctor," he continued, "is still talking about not going back to work until after Christmas, but I intend to return sooner. I can't leave my students in the lurch like this."

Cora stiffened, her own smile falling. Was he insinuating that she couldn't do the job and that he needed to get back to teaching her students? *His,* she reminded herself. "I brought you the seventh graders' essays." She plucked the paper-clipped pages from her bag.

*"Goot, goot,"* he said, accepting them. After he glanced at the one on top, he looked up at her. "Did you go to Jim Mast's with the intention of telling him you wouldn't substitute for me?"

His question so startled her that she froze.

"Did you?" he repeated when she didn't respond. "That Friday when you were late, is that why? Because you went to Mast's first?"

Cora's mind spun. Who had told him that? Certainly not the school board member. She hadn't gone up Jim's lane that day. When she slowed to turn in, she hadn't been able to do it. Had it been God who had led her past the gravel drive to make a U-turn and head for Tobit's house? Had it been her own deep desire to teach? She didn't know. What she *did* know was that she didn't want to discuss the matter with Tobit. Not right now at least, not when she was feeling off-kilter with him. She liked it better when they'd been at odds.

Cora, still not sure what to say to him, met his gaze. Then she did what he had done a few moments before. She redirected the conversation. "*Ach*, before I forget," she said, trying to sound casual. "I decided to go forward with the Christmas program. The students made invitations today to take home to their parents."

Tobit bolted up in the bed. "You did *what*?" he bellowed.

## Chapter Six

Cora met Tobit's fuming gaze. Her first impulse was to respond to his anger with some of her own, but then she thought back to something her mother had told her many years ago. Cora had been fifteen or so and gotten into a minor disagreement with a dear friend, which had quickly escalated to a furious shouting match her friend started. It had been a long time ago and so petty that she couldn't remember the details. What she did remember was that her mother had told her that often when someone became upset about something minor, the anger wasn't necessarily directed to the recipient but to themselves or someone else entirely.

What if Tobit's fury over the Christmas program wasn't about the program? What if his comment about returning to work was about how he felt about himself and not her? Tobit was a widowed man trying to raise a child on his own. Didn't he deserve the same grace she tried to offer others?

It was time for her to let go of her resentment toward Tobit for getting the job she'd wanted. It wasn't like her to hold grudges. And Tobit was a good man, which she'd seen repeatedly in the last two weeks. Yes, he could be gruff with his son and annoyed with his students, but he loved his son and he liked his students. He felt a great responsibility to them and their parents to give the schoolchildren the best education he could.

And how silly was it to be using a Christmas event to get back at Tobit for saying something she might have misinterpreted? The idea was so ridiculous that it was almost funny.

She met Tobit's gaze. Clearly, he didn't think it was funny.

"You had no right to make that decision without me." His face turned red as he raised his voice. "That is my school and those are my students!"

Cora didn't flinch. This man was all bark and no bite. "You're right. I should have consulted with you. I'm sorry."

Not seeming to hear, he talked over her. "When I told you there would be no—" He halted midsentence. "What did you say?"

She kept her tone calm but made it clear she would not be intimidated by his blustering. "I said you're right and I apologize. The Clover school is your responsibility and I'm only here to help until you can return to the classroom. I should have asked you before I made the decision. I didn't bring it up with you again because you already expressed your opinion on the matter." She hesitated and then went on. "But the children and parents were pressuring me. The Christmas program is important to them and they look forward to it all year. If the Clover school doesn't have a holiday presentation, it will be the only one in Honeycomb and that would be a shame, wouldn't it?"

He remained quiet and she could tell that he was calming down. Tobit seemed like a man quick to anger, but he was also quick to release it. Her father had been that way…before his dementia had set in. One minute he would chew out one of his daughters for a chore they'd skipped or naughty behavior; the next he was hugging them and telling them he loved them.

Cora folded her hands in her lap. "Elijah seemed excited about the prospect of the program. He has a very nice singing voice."

Tobit drew back, his surprise replacing any unexpended anger. "You heard him sing?"

Her mouth twitched as she fought a smile. "I did. I let the older children break into groups to discuss what they think should be included in the program and who might be interested in taking the lead on different aspects of the program. I believe the children should organize it themselves. Our upper-grade pupils are old enough to practice time management, leadership and other important skills they can use in their community." She pointed at him. "Your Elijah was the first to speak up and offer to take care of the song selections. He even sang a verse." She brought her hand to her chest. "His voice touched my heart."

"He sang out loud?" Tobit asked in disbelief.

"*Ya*, and then Charlie joined in. The two have a mind to let the boys have a song of their own or switch verses with the girls on some of the selections. And there's talk of a solo. He and Charlie argued all the way here as to which one had the better voice and should do it."

"I can't imagine Elijah taking such initiative," Tobit said with pride in his voice. "He's always been a shy boy." He looked at her. "Well… I guess I can't disappoint him…or our other students."

Cora clasped her hands together in excitement. She knew she'd been taking a chance making the impulsive decision, but she truly believed it would benefit the children and their families. "Really? You don't mind?"

He sighed, leaning back on his pillow. She could see that he was beginning to tire. "*Nay*, I don't mind. So long as I don't have to sing a solo."

She laughed and rose from her chair. "Then it's settled. The children can take their invitations home with them tomorrow."

His forehead creased. "I thought you said they took them home today."

"They *made* them today. I didn't let them take them home. What if you had put your foot down?"

He glanced at her sideways, a look of amusement on his face. "What if I had? I think you'd have gone along with the program anyway. And it would have been the best one in Honeycomb. Will be."

She felt her cheeks grow warm at his compliment. If she didn't know better, she would have thought he was flirting with her. And she liked it. *"Ach,"* she said as she placed her bag on the chair. "I nearly forgot I had something for you."

"For me?"

"For you and Elijah." She pulled a plastic container out of the large canvas tote. "Cookies I made last night with my sisters. We can't keep up with the fresh-baked goods at the store. And it's not only Englishers buying them. We have neighbors and friends who want them, too, which we'd never expected. But all families are busy and don't have the time to make as many home-made treats as they used to. We sell out every day. And the pie orders!" She opened her eyes in amazement, raising her brows as she handed him the container. "We have over forty orders for pie and they're still coming in. If we don't find someone else to bake for us, we'll have to stop accepting the orders." She pointed at the cookie tub. "Oatmeal chocolate chip. Most folks put raisins in them, but I like chocolate chunks, so that's what you got."

He lifted the corner of the lid and inhaled. "I love chocolate in my oatmeal cookies. Better than raisins."

"So much better," she agreed.

"What are all the pie orders for?" Tobit asked, clos-ing the lid container firmly.

She looked at him. "Thanksgiving?" she said, turn-ing it into a question. "Next week."

He frowned. "Thanksgiving is next week?"

"*Ya*, sure is. The last Thursday of November. Every year," she joked. "And a long weekend to go with it. No school Thursday or Friday. That's why we have to begin practice now. The children have agreed to give up some of their recess time so the rehearsals don't in-terfere with schoolwork. Except for Johnny and Noah Mast," she added with amusement. "They thought sac-rificing any time at all was a terrible idea."

He grinned. "Of course those two don't want to give up recess. They need that time to plan their next prac-tical joke."

"Or escape," she said.

"Or escape." He laughed aloud and she joined him.

As their amusement faded, she raised her bag to her shoulder. "What are you and Elijah doing for Thanksgiving? Need a pie?" she teased. "If so, you better order from the Koffman store now."

He shifted his gaze and set the cookies on his nightstand. "No plans," he said, sobering. "We don't do a big dinner."

"Ah. You fast." The moment the words came out of her mouth, she wished she hadn't spoken them. It wasn't appropriate to pry into others' private worship practices. While there were certain requirements for church members, households created their own practices that included communal evening prayer and the celebration of religious holidays. "We know lots of folks who fast for Thanksgiving, but my *dat* grew up in a church in Indiana that wasn't very strict so we never did."

"We don't fast on Thanksgiving."

He looked uncomfortable and she hoped she hadn't offended him. What had gotten into her? She wasn't usually so chatty.

"I'm not exactly in the position to roast a turkey with the trimmings." He pointed toward his leg, which was encased entirely in a brace that looked like a long nylon tube with Velcro fasteners. He had cut off one denim pant leg to accommodate it. "I'm still on bed rest until December first."

Cora chewed on her lower lip. Should she invite Tobit and Elijah to Thanksgiving at their house? She and her sisters planned to cook a turkey, ham and many sides. Elden, Millie and his mother would be joining them as well as Jack and Beth, so everyone was looking forward to the dinner. But with Tobit on bed rest, he wouldn't be able to come, so she said nothing. "I guess I best round up Charlie and get home for chores."

"He's welcome to stay longer," Tobit said. "Elijah likes the company. Unless Charlie's brother is expecting him home for chores. Or Eleanor."

Now that the subject had moved away from the holiday dinner, he looked at ease again. Maybe he didn't like holidays. Perhaps they reminded him too much of his wife and made him sad. Cora felt foolish for not having thought of it sooner.

"I suppose he can stay a little longer," she said. "He has his scooter."

Tobit asked, creases appearing on his forehead, "You didn't take your buggy to school this morning?"

"*Nay.* My sisters needed them and our *dat* took one of the wheels off our wagon again. Henry hasn't had time to repair it." She shrugged. "I have my push scooter."

Tobit met her gaze. "I feel bad that I can't take you home."

"Take me home?" She smiled thinking how sweet that was. But why would he feel the need to drive her home? It sounded almost as if they'd been on a date. "It's been a pleasant day, not too cold or windy. It's been ages since I took a scooter anywhere. I'll enjoy riding home."

As she finished her last words, she noticed he was staring at her. "What?" she said, suddenly feeling self-conscious. She hoped she didn't have any of her lunch on her dress. She and Charlie had leftover chicken and dumpling soup.

He shrugged. "Nothing. I was just thinking—" He

stopped and started again. "I've never known anyone like you, Cora."

She wanted to ask him what he meant. Fearing what he might say, she walked toward the door. "If you could grade those papers, that would be great. I'll pick them up tomorrow. Or the next day," she added. The agreement had been that she would come every other day, but if she visited him again the following day, that would make three times in a row. She didn't know how that would look to her community, which made no sense. They were working together, not dating.

"Anything else for me to grade?" he asked. "Spelling tests, maybe?"

"*Nay.* They're taken care of," she said, not daring to admit that she'd decided to give her suggestion of how to do spelling words a go. They'd had enough disagreement for one day, and she wanted to leave him on a positive note.

"See you Friday." Cora gave him a wave.

"See you Friday," he called. "Thank you."

She glanced over her shoulder to see him smiling.

She returned the smile and hurried out of the house, unsure what had happened. Their relationship had changed in the hour she had been there. She just wasn't sure how.

Feeling guilty that she hadn't helped in the store as often as she should have because of her new job, Cora offered to take Henry's shift on Saturday morning. Henry was working on a bid for a large renovation job for a woman in the Hickory Grove Amish community and she needed time to prepare her proposal. Eleanor wasn't pleased Henry might accept a job that could take months, but she had the good sense not to say anything. Everyone knew their independent-minded sister would do the opposite of what anyone said.

Henry started doing small odd jobs for widows right after their mother died. They had all been so lost that Eleanor, the new head of the household, had encouraged them to find comfort in doing whatever made them happy. In their mourning year, each sister had found solace in some way: Cora had thrown herself into reading fiction and writing for *The Budget*, Millie and Jane had spent hours in the kitchen creating new recipes, Willa had taken over the family's sewing needs and Beth had organized and cleaned every surface in the house.

At first, Henry had struggled to find something to do that would make her smile, but with their father's inability to function as he once had, she began doing things around the house: making repairs, doing paint touch-ups and occasionally putting a hammer to use building a new shelf in the pantry or a closet. The first time a widowed neighbor had asked Henry if she could look at a leaky kitchen faucet, Henry had been unsure if she should. Eleanor encouraged her to go, which Cora suspected her oldest sister had come to regret because soon afterward Henry was asked by others to make house calls. At first, she had done the repairs as a favor. However, when the projects grew bigger and she was offered money for her work, Henry began to accept to contribute to the household finances, which had been sorely lacking until the store opened a few months ago.

Cora glanced up from the cash register. Her job was to ring customers up and keep an eye on their father, who was supposed to be stocking shelves in the store. Mostly he wandered up and down the aisles identifying and sometimes offering commentary on the various items they sold. Right now, she couldn't see him over the freestanding grocery shelves because for some reason, he was down on his hands and knees on the floor.

"Flea and tick spray," Felty Koffman called loudly from the opposite side of the store.

Cora was bagging a customer's pantry items from the bulk foods and the middle-aged woman glanced around, startled.

"De-wormer!"

The woman, who wore an orange ball cap and matching puffy jacket, glanced around trying to figure out where the voice had come from.

Cora smiled as she dropped bags of quinoa and pasta into the reusable bag they sold that read *Willkumm* with a Pennsylvania *Deitsch* hex symbol. The Koffmans weren't Pennsylvania *Deitsch*, but they had second cousins who were, and Jane had insisted that was good enough reason to sell them. Against their family's better judgment, Jane had ordered the bags in bulk, insisting they would sell well, and she had been right. The bags were flying off the counter.

"Currycomb!"

The customer's eyes went round with uncertainty.

"No worries," Cora said, using a phrase she'd heard from one of her older students at school. "That's just my dad stocking shelves."

The woman accepted Cora's two sacks of groceries and looked for the man still calling out the names of merchandise.

"Lice powder!"

Cora pressed her lips together so she wouldn't giggle. "Feel free to pick whichever mum you'd like off the front porch," she told the customer. "The yellow are gone, but there are plenty of nice ones left to choose from."

"Popcorn. In bags and on ears," Cora's *vader* announced.

Shaking her head with amusement, Cora walked out from behind the counter and down the baking goods aisle. She found him on his hands and knees scanning the lower shelves on the next aisle.

"Canned milk! Sweet and unsweetened and something called…*almond milk*. How do you milk an almond?" He looked up at her quizzically. "And why would you?"

Cora laughed aloud. "You don't milk an almond, *Dadi*. I've never done it, but I read that you soak them in water."

He made a face as if he'd tasted something unpleasant. "Why would you want almond milk when we have cows?"

She shrugged good-naturedly. Since her visit with Tobit the day he'd returned from his doctor's appointment, she felt as if she'd stepped out from under a rain cloud that she'd been walking beneath since their mother passed. She couldn't stop smiling. As she had suspected, her relationship with him had changed that day and now she found herself looking forward to visits with him.

"It's an Englisher thing," Cora explained patiently. "We had enough people ask for it that Jane decided we should stock it. It's shelf-stable and it won't go bad, so why not? I guess some people are allergic to milk." She gazed down at him, noting he was wearing his house slippers again but decided not to mention it. "But *Dat*, I thought you were going to put those spices on the shelf. Jane said we've been out of dried rosemary for days."

He sat back with a loud "oof."

"Taking inventory."

"But Jane's already taken inventory. That's how she knew we needed the spices."

"What's Jane done?" Jane walked from the back, into the main room of the shop. She, Beth and Willa were making pies in the store's kitchen in anticipation of the first Thanksgiving order pickups on Monday. The store was filled with mouthwatering scents of baked pumpkin, apple, sweet potato, cinnamon, nutmeg and cloves.

Cora turned to her sister. "I told *Dat* that he doesn't need to take inventory because you already did it." She turned back to him. "All you have to do is take the spices from the boxes and put them on the shelves." She leaned over to demonstrate. "Like this, see?" She picked up a jar of ground cinnamon and added it to the shelf above the proper label.

"No need to tell me how to do my job," he said with annoyance. "I was getting to it." He reached into one of the three small cardboard boxes Jane had carried out earlier, plucked out a jar and slid it onto the shelf.

"*Danki, Dadi*," Jane told him. "Thank goodness we have you. Otherwise, we could never keep up."

The sisters made their way to the counter at the back of the store and Cora walked around to the cash register.

"The pies smell amazing. I hope someone makes one with an ugly crust so we can have it tonight for dessert."

"Not to worry, *schweschter*. I already set two aside for us. Sweet potato, *Dat's* favorite, and apple streusel, Eleanor's favorite. And I gave her an apple to take to Sara's with her."

Cora began arranging a stack of paper bags that had gotten messy on the narrow counter behind her. "*Ach.* I'm glad she went to see Sara. It doesn't sound as if she's doing well."

Eleanor's friend Sara had given birth twice in the last two years, which doctors said had not been good for her diabetes. She'd recently gone into kidney failure and was now on dialysis; the prognosis was not good. Everyone in Honeycomb was praying for her and the family, wishing there was more they could do.

"It's hard to believe she could be so ill," Jane said. "Her Jon is such a good man. Eleanor says he's nearly taken over the care of the babies. Can you imagine a man taking care of babies?"

The bell over the door jingled and Jane glanced over her shoulder to see who it was.

Cora smiled. "*Guder mariye*, Jedidiah."

Jedidiah grinned. "Morning." He was one of Alma and Fred Beachy's nine sons, and perhaps the most handsome. "I wondered if I'd see you here. What with you teaching school now." He strode to the counter and Jane sidestepped to get out of his way.

"Morning, Jed," Jane said as she retreated. Cora had assumed she would return to the kitchen, but instead she hovered in the doorway that led to the back of the building.

"Good morning, Jane." He flashed her a smile and returned his attention to Cora. "On my way back from Dover. *Mam* asked me to get ten pounds of sugar and something called white wheat flour. She said you'd know what that was."

"I'll get them," Jane offered, rushing for the shelves.

*"Danki,"* he told her, then returned his attention to Cora. He wore traditional Amish clothing: homemade denim trousers, a jacket, leather suspenders and a black beanie pulled down over his blond curls. "My uncle and aunt have a singing tonight. I hear they're expecting a big crowd. There's talk of maybe having a bonfire, roasting marshmallows and such. Maybe even…"

Cora crossed her arms, looking up at him, but as he talked, her thoughts strayed. She wondered how Tobit was getting along. It had seemed as if being allowed to get out of bed for a couple of minutes a day to attend to personal needs wore him out and she wondered if he was overdoing it. She didn't dare visit again today because she'd been there every day that week. Maybe she could send Charlie on an errand there to check on him. Charlie and Jack were cutting hay this morning, but she suspected the boy wouldn't be required to work all day. Maybe she could send a pie with him.

"So what do you think?" Jed asked.

Realizing she'd lost track of the conversation, she looked at him. "What do I think?" she repeated.

"About…you know. Letting me drive you home tonight."

*Oh, dear,* Cora thought. What he was asking was the first step in courtship. She wished she'd been paying better attention to what he was saying. How had they gotten from roasting marshmallows to this?

"I...if you're going," Jed added awkwardly.

Cora smiled kindly at him. He was tall but not as tall as Tobit. Handsome, but not as handsome as the teacher. And she had no interest in riding anywhere with him, which was strange because she'd had a secret crush on him for years.

"*Ach*, Jed. Thank you," she said, trying to think quickly. "That's nice of you, but I'll be staying home with our *dat* so my sisters can go to the singing." Plans for the evening hadn't been finalized, at least not for the family, but the moment Jed brought up the event meant to allow young men and women to mix and meet, she knew she had no interest in going.

He looked down at the floor and scuffed his work boot. "Aw, that's too bad. Maybe some other time."

"Here we go, sugar and white wheat flour," Cora said so she wouldn't have to respond to his suggestion to ride with him another time. "*Danki*, Jane." She watched her sister slide one bag and then the other across the counter, then looked up at the young man who seemed more like a boy than a man compared with Tobit. "Does your *mudder* need anything else?"

"That's it." He glanced down at the shelves below the counter that were filled with odds and ends like church keys and electrical tape, but there was also an assortment of candy. "And some peanut butter cups." He grabbed a bag and set it down.

Cora rang Jed up and the moment he walked out the door Jane rushed over. "Why didn't you tell Jed yes? He's so handsome and sweet. I thought you liked him!"

"I do like him," Cora answered carefully. She reached for more grocery bags to occupy her hands. "I just don't...*like* him like him. I don't like him in that way."

Jane tilted her head, her expression one of disbelief. "But every single girl in Honeycomb likes him unless they're already—" She gasped and stared at her sister. "Everyone likes him who doesn't already have a beau," she said slowly. "Which makes me think you have a beau." She sang her last words.

Cora scowled. "I do not have a beau."

"*Oll recht*, fine. You don't have a beau, but you're wishing a certain teacher new to town *was your beau.*" Then she shouted, "Willa! Beth! I was right! Cora likes the teacher!"

"I do not like the teacher," Cora argued, annoyed by her little sister's childish behavior.

"I knew it!" Jane clasped her hands, bouncing in her canvas sneakers. "She likes him!" She hollered. "That's why she's over there all the time *grading papers*!" She turned to their father, who was bringing two empty cardboard boxes to the counter. "Did you know Cora likes Tobit Lapp?"

He handed his youngest daughter the boxes. "I think that's enough teasing," he said quietly. "Could you take these to the back?"

Cora continued to stack grocery bags, keeping her head down. Her face was hot and tears burned the backs of her eyes. She didn't know why she was so upset. She'd certainly teased older sisters over boys in the same way. It was what sisters did.

When Cora and her father were alone, he moved in front of her so that only the counter was between them.

"No need to get angry with Jane," he said gently. "She meant no harm."

Cora said nothing for fear that any response would apparently confirm what the whole family already suspected. Was it that obvious to them that she was developing feelings for Tobit? If it was, could others see it?

"She's young and she's excited to see her big sisters moving on with their lives."

"I know, *Dat*. I'm sorry."

He covered her hand on the counter with his.

Cora rubbed her eyes with the heel of her free hand. "I'm just tired from working all week. And now I have this Christmas program to organize, and stacks of papers to grade and—" She fell silent but didn't remove her hand from his. She thought she was too old for her *dadi*'s comfort, but she realized she wasn't. She also recognized at that moment how much she missed her mother. A girl needed a mother to deal with the feelings stirring inside her.

"Can I tell you something, Cora?"

She looked up at him, a faint smile on her face. This was the *vader* she remembered, the one they saw fewer glimpses of as his dementia progressed. "Of course, *Dat*."

"Maybe it's time you stop fighting *Gott* and let Him do what He does best. Take a breath and see where He's leading you."

He squeezed her hand, let it go, and she watched her father shuffle away in his slippers, thinking perhaps he was right.

# Chapter Seven

By noon on Thanksgiving Day, the Koffman kitchen was a beehive of activity. All the sisters were preparing the holiday meal and enjoying a much-needed day off. Even Beth was there. She, Jack and Charlie had planned to go to the Lehmans' for dinner, but Jack and Charlie's mother had come down with croup and canceled the family meal. While Jack and Elden kept their father-in-law occupied, the women prepared the feast. The twins, Millie and Willa, were setting the table while Eleanor fussed over the turkey gravy. Beth was mixing up a corn casserole, and Jane used beaters for homemade whipped cream for the pies they'd have for dessert. For Cora this was her definition of family. Glorious chaos reigned with everyone talking at once, their voices punctuated by occasional bursts of laughter, spats and the clink and clank of pots, pans, dishes and glasses. To add to the autumn holiday atmosphere, the tantalizing scents of roasted turkey and sweet potato pie hung in the air.

Cora sat across from Henry at the table as they talked

and peeled potatoes from a ten-pound bag. She found it interesting that she and her sisters always searched for ways to be independent of each other, and yet when they were apart, they longed to be together. She reached for another potato. "So that's what's going on with me. I love the job but it's harder than I thought it would be," she admitted.

"That's not a bad thing." Henry tossed a peeled potato into a large stainless colander and reached for another. She liked to use a paring knife, but Cora preferred a peeler.

"*Nay*, I suppose not." Cora smiled. It was good to chat with Henry, who was four years younger than she was.

Of all her sisters, she felt she spent the least time with Henry and she missed her. Though very different from Cora, Henry was a fascinating young woman. Her sister was what folks might call a tomboy, but she had always been complicated. Their mother used to say that talking to Henry was like peeling an onion, but you had to catch her first. She buzzed around like a honeybee, always staying busy, always moving. In the evenings when the other women in their family were knitting or doing crossword puzzles, Henry was cleaning a bridal or repairing a harness. Even as a little girl back when folks still called her Henrietta, her sister preferred outside work and had been good with her hands.

Cora appreciated that Henry hadn't grilled her about Tobit. Since Jane had announced that her big sister liked the Clover school teacher, everyone in her family had been teasing her. It was all in fun, but it was getting on Cora's nerves. She had just begun riding home from events with boys when their mother became ill and romance had taken a back seat to care for her. After their *mam* died, a boy was the last thing Cora was interested in. Now she felt as if she was past the age of wanting to go to bonfires, taffy pulls and such, but that didn't mean she didn't want to meet a man of deep faith, marry and have a family.

"Tell me about the bid you submitted," Cora told her sister. "You said it's for a kitchen renovation?"

Henry's face lit up. She had strawberry blond hair like Cora, but her eyes were blue like their mother's. "I can't believe Edee asked me. Edee Gingerich, I think you've met her before. At the auction last year. They raffled off her quilt and made like a thousand dollars to help cover medical bills in the community. Anyway, she's a friend of Anna Mary's. I've talked with her a bunch of times there. They knit together on Tuesdays."

Cora remembered the quilt but couldn't recall Edee. Anna Mary was a widow in her sixties who lived in Honeycomb; she had been Henry's first paying customer and Henry doted on her now as if Anna Mary were her grandmother. "Wait, isn't she the one who only had two sons and the oldest died and the youngest left the church? I heard she hasn't had contact with the younger one since he walked off the farm. She doesn't even know if he knows his older brother died."

*"Ya."* Henry sighed. "That's what Edee told me. She has two daughters. One lives nearby with a big family, and her husband works as a roofer. The other lives in Indiana. That's why she wants to hire someone to do the construction. Oops!" A potato peel flew off her knife and sailed through the air. She started to rise to retrieve

it when Elden's bulldog darted out from under the table, grabbed the scrap and raced out of the kitchen with it.

Henry laughed as she sat down. "How did he get in here again? I thought Elden put him out on the porch."

Cora gave her a look. "Who do you think might have let him in?"

Their father loved dogs, especially Elden's dog, Samson. The Koffman family dog had passed away the spring before and their *dat* desperately wanted another, but Eleanor insisted it would be too much for him to care for one. Cora didn't agree, but her big sister had so many decisions to make in a day for their father as well as the whole family that she didn't argue with her.

"Elden!" Henry yelled. "Your dog's in the house again."

"Sorry!" Elden hollered from the parlor down the hall. "Get him in a minute. We're having a checkers tournament!"

"I'll get him," Charlie yelled from the back of the house. The pounding of footsteps ensued and the bulldog went through the kitchen and into the mudroom, followed closely by Charlie.

"No running in the house!" Eleanor called after the boy.

Henry sat back down. "Anyway, Edee wants her whole kitchen redone. She wants to go full propane and pull out the wood cookstove."

"She doesn't want it for heat?" Cora reached for the last potato, which was good because her hands were beginning to cramp.

"She has a woodstove in the parlor and her bedroom is downstairs. She says that's plenty of heat for the little house. But she also wants new cabinets and new flooring and the whole walk-in pantry redone." Growing more excited as she talked, Henry gestured with a potato in one hand and the paring knife in the other. "She says nothing has been done to the kitchen since the early eighties when she and her husband moved in. It's a huge job," she gushed, "but I think I'm ready. And she'd be nice to work for."

"Can you do all those things?" Cora asked in amazement.

Henry shrugged and grinned. "I hope we're going to find out. Jack says that if I get the job, he'll be happy to help me any way he can. You know, him being a general contractor." It was Jack who had built their store.

"If you get the job, when will it start?"

"Don't know yet. Probably not until spring." Henry tossed a peeled potato into the colander. "Last one," she declared.

Cora flexed her cramping hands. "Finally."

Henry rose from her chair and picked up the colander. "I'll rinse these off and get them in water." She looked down at Cora mischievously, lowering her voice. "I might even try my hand at boiling them. But don't tell Ellie. Last week she forbade me to cook anything after I burned an entire sheet pan of bacon in the oven."

"I heard that," Eleanor called. Drying her hands on a dish towel, she walked to the table.

Cora stood to take the bowl of peels to the compost pail so Willa and Millie, who were presently fussing over how the cloth napkins should be folded, could finish setting the table.

"Don't forget the salt," Eleanor told Henry as she approached Cora.

Cora stood at the end of the table, bowl on her hip, looking at the beautifully set table set for twelve and bit down on her lower lip, suddenly feeling bad. Here she was, about to enjoy a homemade feast surrounded by those she loved, and Tobit and Elijah were sitting at home alone. She couldn't imagine what they would eat for Thanksgiving, but she had seen his pantry the other day and it was filled with bachelor foods like beef stew, soup and pasta sauce, all in cans. And their refrigerator and freezer were no better: hot dogs, pizza in cardboard boxes and frozen fish sticks.

Eleanor met Cora's gaze, about to say something, and then drew back. "You *oll recht*?" she asked softly enough that no one else could hear her. As if anyone could hear anything. Millie and Willa were now arguing over whether to attempt napkin origami and Jane was trying to explain to Henry how to properly boil potatoes.

Cora sighed and returned her attention to the table. Willa had made the prettiest tablecloth that covered the big farm table they'd added both leaves to, to accommodate their extended family. It was a rich rust color she painstakingly embroidered with the simple outline of leaves in gold, green, orange and yellow. "I was thinking about the Lapps."

"Ah," Eleanor said.

"I feel bad for them—guilty for sitting down to the feast we're preparing," Cora explained. "A single man and his son shouldn't be alone on Thanksgiving eating dinner from a can. I thought about inviting them over but Tobit's still not supposed to be out of bed."

Eleanor nodded. "You're right. It is a shame." She looked down at Cora. "After we eat, do you think you and Charlie should take them plates?"

"Maybe," Cora said slowly, her mind churning. "Or maybe—*nay*, it would be too much." She shook her head. "I couldn't ask everyone to—"

"To what?" Eleanor asked, facing her. "What could you not ask us that we wouldn't do if it was in our power?"

Cora hesitated and then poured out her idea.

Tobit moved slowly down the hall on his crutches. The shower—his first in over two weeks—had felt so good that he'd sat under the steamy mist until he'd emptied the hot water tank. It hadn't been easy sitting with his leg propped on a stool wrapped in plastic outside the shower door, but it had been worth every bit of the fuss. It had sapped his energy, though, and he was looking forward to lying down. He considered taking a brief nap but wondered if that was wise at this time of day since he was already having trouble sleeping.

His restlessness wasn't because he was in pain, which had subsided greatly. It was a petite redhead who was keeping him awake. Since the previous week when he had lost patience with Cora over the school's Christmas program, something had changed between them. They were no longer adversaries, but colleagues.

*Nay*, they were more than that. Friends maybe?

Once he had realized he needed to give up the idea of being in control of everything that went on in his

school while he recuperated, Tobit was able to relax. It quickly had become obvious that even though Cora had no experience as a teacher, she was born to teach. She knew when to be flexible with the students and when to be steadfast. Not only was she knowledgeable, but she knew how to share her knowledge. She knew how to motivate their pupils to help them gain the most from their education as they prepared for the world they would live in as adults.

As much as he hated to admit it, Cora had taught him a thing or two. The previous week they'd again discussed her idea of repeating spelling words on tests until the student got them right. When she'd explained how she would do it by using other students, he had accepted the merits of the idea. While the change hadn't been fully implemented in each grade, he suspected it would greatly benefit their pupils and had given her his blessing.

However, how spelling tests were being administered wasn't what was keeping him awake at night. It was Cora's laughter. It was her unyielding faith in God and the world He had created. It was her thirst for knowledge and love of books. It was the red wisps of hair that framed her heart-shaped face. The silky wisps that, in his dreams, he drew between her fingertips.

His attraction to Cora had taken Tobit by such surprise that he suspected it was partially what made him cantankerous—as she had called him. His attraction to her made him angry with himself. And sad. He didn't want to lie in bed at night and wonder what life could have been for him and Elijah if what had transpired nearly ten years ago hadn't happened. However, if it

wasn't for what had happened in the past, he'd be free
to court Cora. He could have even married her.

But, of course, he couldn't. And if he had any sense
at all, he would set her free to teach on her own and end
her visits, which were supposed to be about him men-
toring her and nothing more. But they weren't and he
suspected Cora knew it, too. She came, not solely because of school, but because she was attracted to him as
well. He saw it in her nutmeg eyes and gentle smile. He
heard it in her voice. The right thing to do would be to
end their personal relationship. But how could he? Right
now, she was the only thing keeping him from falling
into depression over his injury and worse, over the life
he had carefully constructed for himself and Elijah that
wasn't working as well as it once had. He couldn't tell
her not to visit because he couldn't imagine not having
her seated beside him as they graded papers together
and shared an afternoon snack.

At the entrance to the parlor, Tobit halted to catch
his breath. He was about to start forward again when
he heard the distinct sound of buggy wheels on gravel
in the lane. The sound of a second buggy, then a third
followed, and he frowned in confusion. Who could possibly be paying a visit on Thanksgiving Day? Everyone
in Honeycomb should have been seated at their kitchen
table sharing a celebratory meal.

Tobit heard the back door fly open and he flinched
as it hit the wall. He needed to remind his son to be
careful and once he was able, he'd replace the old mal-
functioning doorstop.

"*Dat*! *Dat*, where are you?"

Tobit headed for the kitchen and met his son halfway. "Who's here?"

"The Koffmans! And the Lehmans and the Yoders!" the boy burst loudly with excitement.

Tobit tensed, which caused him to lose balance slightly, and he swayed. Elijah steadied him.

"What are they doing here?" Tobit asked tersely.

"I don't know, but—"

The kitchen door flew open again, struck the wall again, and a moment later was slammed shut. "E!" It was Charlie Lehman. He was the only person who called Elijah that.

"Charlie!" Elijah rushed back into the kitchen.

By the time Tobit made it there, the two boys were trying to snatch each other's knit hats.

"I didn't know you were coming today," Elijah said, giving the Lehman boy a push.

Charlie pushed back. "Makes two of us."

"What's going on, Charlie?" Tobit asked.

The back door opened again, but this time with more control. It was Cora, and against his will, Tobit felt a flush of excitement. He hadn't expected to see her all weekend. But the feeling was quickly replaced by an uneasiness. He was happy to see Cora, but the others? The mere thought of such a big family in his house made him anxious.

"Happy Thanksgiving," Cora greeted with a smile. She wore a black wool cloak and a black bonnet and carried a large red cast-iron pot.

"What are you doing here?" he asked her tersely. "And what's that?"

She strode across the neat kitchen as if it was her

own and placed the pot on the gas stove. "Phew. That's heavy. It's potatoes ready to be mashed," she answered. "I hope you have a masher, otherwise we'll have to make do and use something else."

She whipped off her bonnet and cloak and handed them to the boys as Tobit stood there, frozen, unsure of what to say. What to do.

"Do you want to sit down?" she asked him. "You look pale. The parlor might be a better place than here, though. We've got a lot to do."

Before he could respond, the door opened again. It was Elden's wife, Millie. "Tobit. Good to see you on your feet," she greeted, setting two baskets on the kitchen table. She wore the same outdoor garments as her sister but a blue dress to Cora's rose-colored one. "I hope you're not overdoing it. Elden's afraid you are." She waggled her finger at him. "You fall and break that leg again and you'll be back in the hospital. I'll go for another load," she told Cora. "Come on, boys. Make yourselves useful."

Tobit widened his eyes in disbelief as he watched Millie, followed by the preteens, go out the door. He looked at Cora. "You didn't answer my question," he said, lowering her voice. "Why are you here?"

She rolled her eyes and walked away, pulling a dish towel off one of the baskets. "Because it's Thanksgiving."

He groaned with frustration. "I know it's Thanksgiving! That's not what I asked you."

She looked at him sternly. "No need to raise your voice."

"I'm not raising my voice," he told her. "This is my voice. I'm a big man. I have a big voice."

She pulled a crock of fresh butter out of one of the baskets on the table and the aroma of fresh yeast rolls filled the air. "We're here to have Thanksgiving dinner with you. We decided that if you and Elijah couldn't come to our house, we'd come to yours."

The door opened again; this time it was Elden and, with hot mitts on his hands, he carried an enormous turkey roaster.

"But what if I didn't want Thanksgiving dinner?" Tobit asked.

Elden set the roaster on the stove. "This, my friend, is where you say thank you." He flashed a smile at Tobit. "And enjoy an amazing meal and fellowship. We've got turkey, ham, mashed potatoes, sweet potatoes, applesauce, green beans, roasted turnips, chow-chow, gravy, stuffing and I don't know what else. None of us will need to eat for a week after this meal."

"Should you still be standing?" Cora asked Tobit, setting more items from the baskets on the table and counter. "Elden, maybe you and Tobit should go to the parlor. He's looking a little pale."

Tobit wobbled on his crutches. He'd been on his feet too long and he was beginning to perspire. "I'm all right."

She approached him, a folded rust-colored tablecloth in her arms, and looked up, her brown eyes filled with concern. It was concern for him that he saw and his heart melted. No one had ever looked at him like that before. He would do anything for her. Anything in his power.

"Maybe you should rest for a bit while we get dinner on the table," she told him. "I was hoping you'd feel up to sitting with us. With your foot propped up, of course. Yesterday you said you were tired of eating in bed on a tray and that you wanted to eat at your own table." She opened her arms. "I'd say a Thanksgiving feast is the perfect meal to see how it goes. But if you get tired—"

"I won't get tired," Tobit said softly, unable to take his gaze from hers. *Not sitting next to you.*

"Not to worry," Elden told Cora, tilting his head toward the parlor. "I'll get Grumpy to take it easy for a bit while you prepare the feast."

The back door opened yet again and the rest of the extended Koffman family began to file in carrying dishes and baskets and wooden crates full of food. They all talked at once and the kitchen filled with the sound of voices as it never had and Tobit couldn't help but smile. *Gott* is *goot*, he thought. And for the first time in longer than he could remember, he felt optimistic.

From the porch steps, Cora heard the door open behind her and glanced over her shoulder. She'd come outside to get a breath of fresh air before she helped her sisters pack up the buggies to go home. Tobit's kitchen was smaller than theirs at home, and while it was able to accommodate all fourteen of them, between the warmth of the stovetop and oven and all the people, she'd gotten overheated.

A hulking shadow filled the doorway.

"Tobit," she said, rising. "You should be resting."

He balanced on his good foot, pulled the door closed behind him and made his way across the white clap-

board porch on his crutches. "Lots of things we should do that we don't, like you shouldn't be so bossy."

His tone was teasing, and she smiled and eased down on the top step. She watched as he leaned his crutches against the rail and slowly eased his way down until he sat beside her. "Be careful. You're going to—" She closed her mouth. Tobit was a grown man. He was right; she shouldn't be so bossy with him.

When he settled beside her, she looked at him and then gazed into the dark barnyard. It felt strange to feel him close; when she visited him, he was always in the bed with her in the chair with space between them. They weren't touching now, but she felt the heat from his body and smelled his shampoo.

Crossing his arms over his chest, he leaned back and stared into the dark. The stars sparkled in the night sky. They were quiet for a while, enjoying the cool night air and twinkles of mystery in the canopy overhead.

"This might be the nicest thing anyone has ever done for me," Tobit said, his words sounding as if they were as much for him as for her.

"What? Brought you dinner?" She laughed, feeling nervous with him so near. It wasn't a bad nervousness. It felt good but also very unfamiliar. "I don't believe that."

"Cora, you didn't simply drop off dinner. You up-ended your whole family. You set my table and finished cooking your meal here. You included Elijah in your family's celebration." He locked gazes with her. "You even convinced Elden's mother to come with you."

"Oh, she wouldn't have missed this for the world. I guarantee you that. She's been dying for weeks to pay a visit and bring you a pan of rice cereal bars."

"Hmm. I like rice cereal bars."

"*Ya*, but Lavinia comes with them, and knowing you, I doubt you'd have much patience for her."

"I can deal with Lavinia just fine, *danki*. I'll growl at her." He growled at Cora, baring his teeth and making his hands look like claws.

She rocked back and grinned. "Be careful, she might growl back."

He cut his blue eyes at her. "Or bite me."

They laughed together and she said, "That's unkind of me. She's Millie's mother-in-law and now that I know her better, I kind of like her. Her heart is always in the right place, but she likes to get into other people's business."

"Like someone else I know."

She smirked and pushed his shoulder with hers. It was a gesture she might have made to one of her sisters but the moment they touched, it felt different. She turned to look at him, only to find him studying her, and it crossed her mind that it would be so easy for him to kiss her right now.

He lowered his head ever so slightly and she knew he was thinking the same thing.

"I should go inside," she whispered.

His nod was barely noticeable. He cleared his throat. *"Ya,"* he agreed.

Cora popped up and rushed for the door, wondering if this tightness in her chest was love.

## Chapter Eight

"We wish you a merry Christmas," Willa and Jane sang loudly.

"And a happy new year," Cora chimed in as she dipped an ice cream scoop into the cake batter and dropped it into a cupcake paper in a pan.

They had opened the store that morning at 6:00 a.m. and offered a few specials to coincide with the Englishers' "Black Friday." However, they closed early with the intention of having the same schedule the following day. Because none of them had to work for the rest of the day, Millie had invited her sisters to her house to bake. They had all come except Henry, who was at Edee Gingerich's house repairing a washing machine.

The Koffman sisters were making cakes and cupcakes to go into the store's freezer. They would be removed and decorated so they could sell them fresh Christmas week. The sisters were also making frosting to freeze to speed up the process. Then they could easily thaw what they needed and assemble, frost and decorate the cakes quickly. Jane's plan was for some of the cakes and cupcakes to be decorated with Christmas sprinkles in red and green or silver and gold. Others would be adorned with fresh greenery items Jane insisted would be popular. They'd baked lemon, almond, chocolate and vanilla cakes. Then various flavored frostings could be used interchangeably. Chocolate ganache and the lemon and raspberry fillings would be made when Christmas was closer.

"Last two pans of the lemon cupcakes going into the oven," Cora announced when they ended the song. She grabbed a hot mitt off the butcher-block counter and slid both pans onto an oven rack in Millie's massive eight-burner cookstove. She set a white timer to twelve minutes so she wouldn't overcook them. "That makes two hundred and forty cupcakes."

"Two hundred and thirty-nine," Millie corrected. "I dropped one on the floor and Samson got to it before I did."

Jane laughed. "Holly leaf paper and all." She stood at the counter beside Cora and scraped fluffy white buttercream frosting from a mixing bowl into a plastic container suitable for the freezer. "I hope it doesn't make him sick."

"Trust me. It won't," Millie assured her. "The other day I dropped a hardboiled egg while I was making egg salad for Elden and he swallowed the whole thing in one gulp, shell and all."

"Elden ate the egg with the shell on it?" Jane asked, wide-eyed.

Millie giggled. "*Samson* ate it off the floor, not Elden."

Everyone joined in the laughter and Cora's heart soared. She was having such a good Thanksgiving week, the best she'd ever had. School had gone smoothly from Monday to Wednesday and then they had such a joyful Thanksgiving Day.

She still couldn't believe she'd rounded up the entire family to take their meal to Tobit and Elijah, but she was glad she had. Elijah had been beside himself with excitement to have a houseful of people, especially because Charlie had been able to make it. And once his shock that they were there wore off, Tobit had been equally happy, although his response was more subtle. And the best part of the day was when Cora had been alone with Tobit gazing at the stars. When she closed her eyes, she could still feel the warmth of his body close to hers. She wondered if she had stayed put if Tobit would have tried to kiss her. The bigger question was, would she have let him? Cora wanted to think she'd have said no. A woman wasn't supposed to kiss anyone but her husband, but times were changing. Maybe she would have dared a quick kiss.

*"Schweschter?"*

Cora heard giggling and her eyes flew open. She'd been daydreaming about Tobit. She felt her cheeks grow warm.

"Did you hear me?" Beth stood in front of her with a hand on her hip. "I said that Jack and I thought you looked awfully cozy with Tobit on his back step last night."

"You were spying on me from the window?" Cora asked, mortified.

"Not from the window. We'd gone for a walk." Beth pressed her lips together as if fighting a smile. "A romantic walk."

Jane snickered and covered her mouth.

"It's what newlyweds do," Beth told her little sister, swinging around to peer at Jane. "You'll see one day." She returned her attention to Cora. "We practically walked right by you two and you didn't notice us. Neither one of you," she added with a smirk. "Did he ask you out finally?"

"Ask me out where?" Cora carried the mixing bowl to the large porcelain farmhouse sink.

Millie had a beautiful kitchen with updated appliances, plenty of cabinets and a sturdy butcher-block countertop. The room was high-ceilinged with big windows on two sides and had recently been painted a pale blue, Millie's favorite color, because Elden wanted his wife to feel at home in her new house.

Cora squirted dish soap in the bowl and turned on the faucet, scrubbing with a sponge. "Tobit isn't going out anywhere. He hasn't been out of the house since his accident, except to go to doctor's appointments."

"You know very well what I mean," Beth said. She snapped a dish towel and took the mixing bowl from Cora when the suds were rinsed off. "He's obviously attracted you. And all you talk about is Tobit this, Tobit that. What's taking you so long? Neither of you is a spring chick."

Cora felt her face grow hotter. Cora was older than Beth and Millie, and although she didn't come out and say it, Beth was referring to having a family.

"You *have* been seeing each other for weeks," Eleanor pointed out as she wrapped cooled cake layers in plastic for the freezer.

"We haven't been *seeing* each other," Cora argued.

"I'm teaching his classes for him. I…we have things to talk about."

"Every day?" Willa teased. "Sounds like you're *seeing* each other every day to me."

Cora collected more dirty dishes. They were winding down with their baking and it soon would be time to clear out of Millie's kitchen. Her sister wanted to make kielbasa and sauerkraut for supper for her, Elden and her mother-in-law, who ate with them most nights.

"If he hasn't asked you," Jane said, stacking clean cake pans in a wooden crate to return to the store's kitchen, "why don't you ask him."

Eleanor cut her eyes at Jane. "It's not how we do things," she said firmly. "A man is in charge in a relationship and he asks a woman. Not the other way around."

"But what if he's shy?" Jane raised both hands in the air, gesturing dramatically. "It's obvious he likes her. But maybe it's been a long time since he asked a woman out. Cora said he's been widowed for years. Since Elijah was little. What if he's scared to ask Cora out?"

"I have an idea," Millie said, her excitement matching Jane's. "Why don't you go with him tomorrow to shop for Elijah's birthday present? Elden has already hired the van to take them."

"They're going shopping?" Cora asked. She turned from the sink and grabbed a dish towel to dry her hands. "I didn't know about that."

"They discussed it yesterday while we were putting the finishing touches on dinner. Tobit was upset about not having a birthday gift for Elijah. He turns thirteen in a few days. Anyway," Millie went on, "Elden suggested they go someplace where they have those battery cart things. That way Tobit can ride around, find a gift and get what groceries and such he needs all in one trip." She put her hands together, interlacing her fingers. "Please, won't you go with Tobit so Elden doesn't have to? I want to attend the couples' luncheon Elden's Uncle Gabriel's church is sponsoring. Beth and Jack are invited, too. But Elden forgot about the event when he was talking to Tobit and now he feels like he can't let his friend down. Or Elijah."

Cora nibbled on her lower lip in thought. The idea was tempting. She could certainly assist Tobit and maybe Charlie could join them. They could make a day of it. She needed to buy supplies for their students at the craft store, anyway. Each grade had been assigned a decoration to make their schoolroom look festive, and they would also make Christmas cards. "I don't know," she said slowly. "You think Tobit would want me to go when he already has plans with Elden?"

Millie made a face that suggested Cora was being ridiculous. "Would a single man rather go shopping with his guy friend? Or a pretty girl he's sweet on? Really, *schweschter*, you have to ask?"

"You should go," Jane insisted. "It would be such a fun day." She looked over her shoulder at their eldest sister. "She should go, shouldn't she, Eleanor?"

Eleanor stacked several layers of wrapped chocolate cake in the cardboard box they'd use to transport the baked items across the road to the store. "I think it would be fine to offer to go with Tobit. And it would be nice if Millie and Beth could attend the luncheon with their husbands." She turned to Cora. "I will say that I'd advise you to take Charlie and Elijah with you. You have been spending a lot of time with Tobit and you don't want people gossiping about you."

"What Ellie means," Willa said as she licked frosting from a beater, "is that she doesn't want Aunt Judy to come to the house and tell her she's letting us run wild. Last week she complained because she saw me talking with one of the Beachy boys after church without a chaperone."

"Which Beachy?" Jane piped up.

"Not telling," Willa answered, sticking her tongue out at her sister.

Jane copied the gesture.

Eleanor ignored them both. "I'm not saying you've done anything inappropriate, Cora. I'm only suggesting that if you think you'd like to court Tobit, and I hope you do, you have to be careful. You don't want to appear to be doing anything inappropriate. You know how tongues wag."

"Aunt Judy's, maybe," Jane murmured.

Eleanor gave Jane a look that suggested she was out of line, and the teenager mouthed "Sorry."

Cora's timer went off for her cupcakes and she hurried to the oven. Did she dare offer to go with Tobit in Elden's stead? Was she brave enough to be so forward?

She smiled to herself as she slipped hot mitts over her hands. She thought maybe she was.

Cora walked beside Tobit down the aisle at Walmart pushing a full grocery cart. He'd been apprehensive about driving the battery-powered scooter, but he'd quickly gotten the hang of it, and they'd had a good laugh over his backing-up skills.

The previous evening Elden had gone to Tobit's and suggested the change of plans to accommodate his new wife. According to her brother-in-law, Tobit had been pleased and perhaps even eager about Cora going in his place. At one o'clock, the hired Mennonite driver picked Cora and Charlie up and then Tobit and Elijah. It had taken Tobit a few minutes to get into the van, but he had managed. She was fascinated by his strength and how easily he'd maneuvered himself onto the van's middle seat so his leg was supported.

The boys accompanied Cora into their first stop, a craft store, while Tobit stayed in the van with the driver. Then because they were all hungry, they'd gone to Chick-fil-A for chicken sandwiches, fries and peppermint milkshakes. It was only the second meal Cora had shared with Tobit and the first one-on-one meal with him after Charlie and Elijah asked permission to sit by themselves. As she and Tobit ate their lunch, they chatted about school, the upcoming Christmas program, the Koffmans' store and other things. They discussed their favorite books, and Tobit provided a glimpse of his sad childhood when he told her about his uncle banning books in the house after he caught Tobit reading with a flashlight when he should have been asleep. The fact that Tobit willingly discussed the painful memory with her made Cora's heart swell. This man was the kind she had dreamed of marrying, one who was strong when he needed to be but was able to be vulnerable at times.

Sitting across from each other, sharing a meal with Christmas music playing over the loudspeakers, Cora had imagined what it would be like to court Tobit. To have him as her husband. Because he had a child, she knew there would be few dates with only the two of them. Still, she found herself oddly comfortable including Elijah and Charlie in their outing. Maybe she didn't mind others on what could be seen as a date because she came from a big family and rarely went anywhere without one of her sisters or her *dat*. Or maybe it was because she already saw Tobit as a family man, so it was logical that they would include Elijah and his friend.

The superstore was their last stop. Once the driver dropped them off at the door, the boys brought the scooter to Tobit and the four grocery-shopped together. Goofing around with the preteens, Tobit showed her a lighthearted side of himself. The boys put items into the cart and Tobit, gruffly protesting, removed them. In the end, though, the cart was filled not just with necessities but also snacks and new socks and gloves, and two coffee mugs Elijah had spotted. The boy had started drinking coffee since he learned to make it, and Elijah wanted him and his father to have matching mugs, which she thought was adorable. What was more delightful was that Tobit went along with it to please his son. Once the groceries were in the cart, Charlie asked if he and Elijah could go off alone to see the fish for sale in tanks, a ploy planned ahead of time. Tobit played along and soon he and Cora were alone.

"You think he'll like the blue fishing rod?" Tobit fretted. He stopped the battery-powered cart in an aisle with no other customers. "Maybe he'd like the green one better. The green pole and the blue tackle box."

"I think he'll be tickled with what you got him, but

we can go back and change them out if you like." They
were in the household aisle and Cora picked up a candle
in a glass jar candle, lifted its wooden lid and sniffed.
"Mmm. Smells good," she said. She looked at the label.
"Balsam and cedar. Smells like Christmas. Try it." She
held it under his nose.

He breathed deeply. "It does smell good. Add it to
the cart."

She lifted her brow. She'd never seen a candle in his
house. His home was austere and neat as a pin, but there
was nothing inside it that wasn't a pure necessity except
for Elijah's graded school papers that were proudly dis-
played on the refrigerator with magnets. "Really? You
want this?" she asked him.

He shrugged. "What? A man can't like a nice scent
in his home?"

She met his gaze. He smiled and she returned his
smile. "You are a man full of surprises, Teacher."

"How's that, Teacher?"

It was a thing that had begun that morning and carried through the day. She'd called him Teacher to tease
him and he'd repeated it whenever he addressed her. It
was silly but it amused them…and caused the boys to
look at each other in puzzlement.

"I don't know." Cora crossed her arms. She'd worn
her black wool cloak because it was a cold day but it
was in the shopping cart. The store was packed with
holiday shoppers and warm enough that she'd rolled up
her sleeves to her elbows. "Maybe because you give the
impression of being the big, burly, cranky bear." She
chuckled. "But now I see you're just a big cub—who
likes matching coffee mugs and scented candles."

He narrowed his gaze. "I'm not sure if I should take that as a compliment."

She rested her hand next to his on the steering bar of his cart. The store was filled with loud voices and Christmas music, punctuated by announcements, yet it suddenly felt as if he and she were alone. She'd gotten the same impression two nights earlier when they'd gazed at the stars. "I meant it as a compliment," she said quietly.

He studied her hand and then moved his until their fingers touched and she felt warmth spreading from her belly through her entire body. *Was this what it felt like to fall in love?*

Tobit pulled his hand away suddenly. "We best go. I want to pay for the birthday gifts and have you put them in the back of the van before Elijah sees them." He turned the knob on the handlebar that gave the cart power and pulled forward, leaving her behind.

Cora stood there for a moment, unsure of what had just happened. They'd had such a good day that she'd begun to imagine Tobit asking to court her formally and then their wedding like Beth's and Millie's that her family had just celebrated.

Had she misinterpreted Tobit's intentions toward her? Had she thought he had feelings for her when he didn't? It was possible, but her sisters all had said the same thing. They believed Tobit was going to ask her out. Eleanor had even made a joke at the Koffman supper table the previous night about another wedding possibly in the wind.

"You coming?" he called over his shoulder without looking at her.

Her eyes felt scratchy like she was about to cry. "Coming!" she said, pushing the heavy grocery cart.

An hour later, the groceries were unloaded in Tobit's kitchen and Charlie had managed to sneak Elijah's birthday gifts out of the van and into a closet. The driver had left to run an errand to give Cora time to help Tobit put groceries away, but they were expecting her back within the hour. The boys had gone outside to feed the animals but promised to keep watch for their ride.

"Last item," Cora said, pulling the Christmas candle out of a paper bag. She raised the lid to sniff it again and the pleasant evergreen aroma drifted through the room. "Where would you like it?"

Tobit looked up. He sat at the kitchen table, folding the bags. She intended to take them all to school on Monday for a project for her fourth graders. They were going to cut them down to make envelopes for the homemade cards they would be making for the widows and widowers of Honeycomb. It was a tradition at the Clover school dating back to when Cora attended.

When Tobit didn't answer, she set the new candle on the table. He picked it up. "It's for you." He offered it.

"Me?" Now she was really confused. Tobit had been so sweet all day, even flirty at times. Then when his hand touched hers, everything changed. He'd not been unkind or raised his voice since then, but he'd been cool with her. He and the boys had sat in the back of the minivan while she'd taken the passenger's seat up front with the driver. Tobit had talked with the boys all the way home, leaving her out of their conversations. And now he was giving her a gift? "It's for me?" she asked. "But I thought you liked it."

"I do." He pushed the candle toward her. "I like it for you."

Cora slowly accepted the candle, her mind flying in multiple directions at once. She was hurt by his cool behavior and annoyed at the same time by his puzzling signals. "Tobit, what's going on here?" she blurted before she could stop herself.

"Going on?" he echoed. "What do you mean?"

She felt her face heating up and again her eyes were scratchy. *Just be quiet,* she told herself. *Say thank you and walk away.* As Eleanor had said, the man was supposed to be the one to direct a relationship.

But were they in a relationship? And even if they were, why did the male always get to control every situation? Shouldn't women have a say, too?

Cora knew the smart thing was to go home. Go home right now and drop the subject. But she couldn't do it. "Are you going to make me say it?" she asked.

He stared at her and she groaned and closed her eyes for a moment. When she opened them, he was still looking at her.

"Between us, Tobit." She motioned to him and then to herself with her free hand. "What is going on here?"

He frowned. "Nothing is going on between us. I don't know what you mean."

She took a step back, embarrassed. "I'm sorry," she managed. "I... I guess I misunderstood. I thought... I thought you liked me. I thought we liked each other and maybe—" Tears threatened to spill. "I should go," she said, turning away so he wouldn't see her cry.

She was almost out of the kitchen when he called her name. He sounded as if he was in pain and as miserable as she felt. "Cora, wait. There…there's been no misunderstanding. I do like you."

Her breath caught in her throat and she turned to face him. "You do?"

"I do. And there's nothing I'd like more than to walk out with you. Marry you," he said, his voice filled with more emotion than she'd ever heard from him. "But, Cora, I'm married."

Relief flooded her. He liked her! He said he wanted to marry her! And suddenly her heart was pounding in her chest. "You were married. Right. Widowed." She hugged the gift he had given her. "I know. And you're older than me, and you have Elijah to think about, but—"

"*Nay*, not widowed," he interrupted, lowering his gaze until he stared at the oak table. "Elijah's mother… my wife, Aida, she…she's not dead, Cora. I… I'm still married."

# Chapter Nine

As Tobit watched, the color drained from Cora's cheeks and her eyes filled with tears. The knowledge that he'd caused her pain broke his heart, a heart he'd thought could never break again because it was already broken. The difference, however, was that when his wife had left him and Elijah, Aida had been the one who had caused the devastation. The pain that radiated in his chest now was a result of his own doing.

How could he have let this happen? How had he let his deception go on for so long that now he was harming others?

He was responsible for his and Cora's pain. He'd been misleading others for so long that he had almost come to believe his lies. He told the story so many times that in day-to-day life, he *saw* himself as a widower. And it had worked well until he came to Honeycomb. Until he met Cora. In the past, it had never mattered that he wasn't free to marry because he'd had no interest in marrying again. All he wanted was to be a good father to Elijah and somehow make up for the fact that his son's mother had left him. But then he had met Cora and dared to consider what it would be like to have her for his wife. His mind had known it could never be, but his heart had let things go too far. He'd allowed her to care for him as much as he cared for her.

"Married," she murmured, wiping at her eyes with the heel of her hand.

He hung his head in shame. *"Ya."*

"Your wife isn't dead?"

*"Nay."*

Cora clutched the scented candle he'd given her. The faint scent of balsam and cedar still hung in the winter air and he remembered the way she had smiled when she had smelled it in the store. He liked doing things to make her smile, but now he feared she would never smile at him again.

"I'm sorry," he said, forcing himself to look at her. "I never meant to hurt you. I do care for you. A great deal, but—" But what? There was no excuse for what he had done. The loneliness he had felt for so many years, the pain and the frustration of his injury were no justifications for doing this to Cora. To his beautiful, smart, kind Cora.

She took a step back from him, appearing more shocked than angry. "But I don't understand. When you came to Honeycomb, you told everyone that your wife had died. That she'd been gone nearly ten years. And it was a lie?"

"Yes. No." He squeezed his eyes shut. "It was part truth, part untruth." He opened them again. "She *has* been gone almost ten years. But she didn't die." His voice caught in his throat. "She left us."

Cora took a deep breath. She looked so small and vulnerable that he had an inexplicable desire to take her in his arms. Of course, he couldn't. Not ever because his wife was out there somewhere. When he and Cora had touched today in the store, he had realized that.

"What do you mean your wife *left* you?" she asked.

He forced himself to look at her and shrugged. "I mean she left. I went to work one day. I was teaching in a small Amish community in Chautauqua County where we lived in upstate New York. When I came home, she and Elijah were gone."

Cora drew back in disbelief. "She took him? Then how—"

"*Nay*, she didn't take him with her." He drew his hand across his mouth. A few minutes ago he had been hungry and Cora had told him an easy way to make lasagna on the stovetop. Now he felt like he might be sick. Even after a decade, he could still feel the hurt and confusion he had experienced that day. "She walked to the neighbor's and left him with some made-up excuse. We never saw her again."

Cora held the candle tightly against her. "She left her *baby*?"

He nodded. "Elijah had just turned three."

"But where did she go? How did she—" Cora's eyes teared up again. "I'm so sorry, Tobit," she whispered. "I can't imagine what that must have been like for you." Her face hardened. "But…but why would you lie about something like that? Why did you tell us you were widowed? Why did you let me think—"

Her voice trembled and she didn't finish her thought,

but she didn't have to. Her expression told him. *Why did you let me believe you were a single man?*

He drew his thumb along the edge of a paper bag he'd folded for use in their classroom. "For months after Aida left, I thought she'd come back so when Elijah asked for her, I—" His voice cracked and he paused. Once he had regained control of his emotions, he continued. "At first, I told Elijah she was sick. That she was at the hospital and that she'd come when she was better. I told our friends and neighbors the same thing." He leaned back in his chair, letting his hands fall to his lap. "After six months, when I didn't hear from her and she didn't return, I realized she was never coming back. I sold our place. I told Elijah she died and we moved to Wisconsin, where no one knew us or Aida. I did it because…not because I didn't care if people thought I was such a terrible husband, but because I didn't want Elijah to know that his mother hadn't loved him enough to stay."

She was quiet for a moment and then said, "And you never heard from her again? From her family?"

He shook his head slowly. "I never met them. She and her parents were estranged."

"And they didn't know where she'd gone when you asked?"

His gaze fell to the hardwood floor. It needed to be swept. Elijah had spilled cereal that morning and forgotten to sweep it up or let the dog in to clean it up for him. "I couldn't find them."

"So you never tried to find out where she'd gone?" she demanded, raising her voice to him. It seemed as if her shock had passed and now she was angry. Angry at him. And she had every right to be, but that didn't make it sting any less.

"*Nay*, I didn't look for her, Cora," he answered firmly. "She left me. She left us. No note. Just her prayer *kapp* on our bed." The pain of that memory washed over him, threatening to drown him. All these years he'd told himself it was his fault she'd gone and that he had to make it up to Elijah. "Before we moved, I went to the mailbox every day for weeks, for months, hoping to hear from her. Praying that she would at least tell me why she'd abandoned us. But no letter came because she didn't want to come home or be found."

"She left her *kapp*, so she didn't want to be Amish anymore?"

He raised his hands lamely. "I have no idea. I… I guess. I knew she was unhappy. She never took to mothering or to being a wife, but she never said anything about leaving the church." He exhaled. It had been so long ago that it was hard for him to recall all the details. Maybe because he'd pushed to make himself forget for so long.

"So this is why you've moved so often," Cora said slowly. "So no one would know. And that's why you've always kept to yourself. To prevent folks from asking too many questions."

"I did it to protect Elijah. To protect my son from the knowledge that his mother abandoned him. Thinking back now, maybe it wasn't the right thing to do. But it's what I did. I was hurt and I was ashamed, Cora." He met her gaze. "I was ashamed that I couldn't take care of my wife, that she didn't want to be with me or our son." He clasped his hands together. "But you have to believe me when I tell you that I did it for our son, not me."

When she said nothing, he went on. "I can't tell you how sorry I am, Cora. It was wrong for me to let myself care for you. It was wrong of me to let you think that I was free to court you because I'm not." He took a deep breath. "I wish that I was, but I'm not."

"No, you're not," she answered stiffly. "And in your deceit, you led me to wrong your wife because gone or not, you are still wed to her."

A silence stretched between them and Tobit stared at the paper bags on the table. The ache in his leg from the activity of the day throbbed. He couldn't think of anything to say that would make Cora understand how sorry he was that he had lied to her. And to everyone in Honeycomb who had been so kind to him and Elijah and welcomed them into their community. How unhappy he was that he couldn't court her and marry her.

Cora was the first to speak. "You have to tell him, Tobit." Her voice became stronger with each word. Resolute. "You have to tell your son the truth."

"I don't know if I can. What if he hates me?"

"He's a smart boy. He'll be angry, but he loves you. Eventually, he'll understand that you made a terrible mistake, and everyone makes mistakes—"

His head snapped up to look at her. "This isn't a mistake like marking a correct answer wrong in haste, Cora! This is… It's unforgivable."

*"Nay,"* she said firmly. "Nothing is unforgivable. Not with *Gott*. But you can't keep living this lie. It's hurting you. You must tell Elijah and your bishop. You must confess and ask for *Gott's* forgiveness."

He laughed without humor. "Confess to whom? I don't have a bishop. I haven't chosen a church district yet. Before my accident, we attended different churches. I was still figuring out which district best suited us when I broke my leg."

"Then talk to my uncle, Bishop Cyrus. He's a good man and he'll know what to do. How to help you."

The back door flew open, startling them both.

"Van's here!" Charlie announced. He looked back and forth between Cora and Tobit. "Something wrong?"

*"Nay."* Cora rubbed her eyes. "Just tired." Still holding the candle he'd gifted her, she took her cloak from the back of a chair and walked out of the house.

Tobit wanted to call out to her to come back. He wanted to talk more with her, but what else could he say? He had wronged her and there were no words that could repair the damage.

The kitchen was blessedly quiet as Cora walked into her house and set her bags of purchases on the table. Charlie, no doubt guessing that something bad had happened between her and Tobit, mumbled something about getting an early start on homework before he made a quick retreat upstairs to his bedroom.

Listening to his footsteps on the stairs, she hung up her cloak and put the paper towels in the pantry. Only the light over the stove glowed but she didn't turn on another. The gloom well suited her mood.

Unsure of what to do, Cora stood at one of the windows, staring into the dark barnyard. The house was strangely quiet even though it was only seven in the evening, and she wondered where everyone was. She felt numb from head to toe. Her mind flickered from one thought to the next without focusing on any one thing. The kitchen she loved felt unfamiliar. It was peculiar how one event could change how you saw yourself and the world. She'd felt something similar the day of her mother's death. The realization made her feel guilty because how could the experiences be compared? Why did she feel this overwhelming sense of loss? She and Tobit hadn't courted.

The thought of his name made her lower lip tremble and tears filled her eyes.

"Cora?" Eleanor called from somewhere in the house.

Cora couldn't find her voice to respond.

The appeal was followed by her oldest sister's distinct gait. Eleanor never dragged her prosthetic leg, but there was the slightest scuff in her stride. With the house rarely this quiet, Cora had forgotten the sound.

"There you are," Eleanor said as she walked into the kitchen. "Why are you in the dark?" She flipped a light switch and the room was bathed in soft light.

Cora heard the clink of a glass being set down in the porcelain sink.

"*Dat's* tucked in bed with a farming magazine to read. He went down without a fuss for once. It was his idea to go early." The faucet squeaked as Eleanor turned it on and the sound of water followed. "He went with Jack to a job site this afternoon and they moved lumber." She continued. "Jack wore him out, bless him."

Cora stood stiffly, her back to her sister. She was trying hard not to cry because once started she'd never be able to stop them. Early in the day, she'd left this kitchen with such high hopes. She had been looking forward to spending time with Tobit…and with Elijah and Charlie.

*"Schweschter?"* Eleanor's voice broke into Cora's thoughts.

Cora couldn't move as if her feet were stuck to the floor. And she couldn't speak with the huge painful lump in her throat.

"Cora?" Eleanor crossed the kitchen and laid her hand on Cora's arm.

Cora turned to look at Eleanor and her sister's face fell.

*"Ach*, what's the matter? What's happened?" Eleanor asked, her voice filled with concern.

When Cora didn't answer immediately, Eleanor took her by the hand and led her to the kitchen table. "Sit. I'll make us some tea. Have you eaten?"

Cora sat and turned her head one way and then the other. "I don't think I can eat," she whispered.

Eleanor crouched down to study her features. "I heard Charlie go into the bathroom for his shower. Is he all right?"

Cora nodded.

Eleanor held her gaze. *"Goot.* I saved you some supper. It's only leftover chicken potpie. The girls went to the Masts' for a bonfire and chili. But if you don't want that, we can have some cookies. You look a little piqued, like my friend Sara when her blood sugar gets too low."

Eleanor moved about the kitchen as she made a pot of tea and set out a plate of sweets. She gathered their mother's favorite teacups rather than their everyday mugs. As a little girl, Cora had always loved the china pattern with its red strawberries and green leaves.

After everything was prepared and on the table, Eleanor sat in the chair next to Cora. She poured two cups of tea, giving one to Cora, and then placed the serving plate of beautifully decorated Christmas cookies between them.

Cora finally felt able to talk. "I need to resign from my position at the school," she said, her voice sounding unfamiliar.

Eleanor hesitated and then said, "And why would you do that?" She sighed and brushed her hand across Cora's back as she leaned to put out two small dessert plates. "Please don't tell me you and Tobit quarreled again. Honestly, I'm beginning to think the two of you are as alike as two peas in a pod."

"We didn't quarrel," Cora murmured. "Not really."

Eleanor studied Cora's face as she added a heaping spoon of sugar into each of the teacups. "Drink," she said, indicating the cup with a lift of her chin.

Cora obeyed. The tea was hot and strong and sweet.

"Have a cookie."

When Cora didn't respond, Eleanor plucked several off the serving plate and put them on Cora's. "A sugar cookie, a cream cheese spritz and a peanut butter chocolate chip. Have a bite."

Cora stared at her plate of cookies.

"Listen to me," Eleanor said. "I can't help you if you don't tell me what's wrong. So say it. You'll feel better for sharing your burden. I promise."

Cora took a deep breath. "I won't be seeing Tobit anymore. And I don't think I can—" Her voice caught in her throat and came out as a squeak. "I don't think I should teach his classes," she managed.

"And why's that?"

Cora wrapped both hands around her teacup, savoring the heat, but didn't raise it to her lips. "I can't tell you," she whispered.

Eleanor leaned closer. "I'm sorry. I didn't hear that."

"I can't tell you," she repeated louder. "It wouldn't be right to talk about Tobit's business."

"Wouldn't be right?" Eleanor demanded. "He's obviously hurt you. I think I have the right to know what he's done to you. Did he tell you to keep quiet?"

Cora indicated no.

Eleanor was silent for a moment. "I promise you that no one will hear a word from me. Not even our sisters, if that's your wish."

Cora didn't know what to do. It didn't seem right to tell Tobit's secret. It was his to tell, but she was falling apart inside. She had to tell someone. She couldn't keep the pain to herself. It was too big.

Her sister sipped her tea.

Cora did the same, then she picked up the smallest cookie, a lemon spritz that was her favorite, and took a tiny bite. "He's married, not widowed," she said.

"He's *what*?" Eleanor looked shocked, then angry.

Cora flinched and her sister laid her hand on her back. "I'm sorry," Eleanor apologized. "My tone wasn't meant for you. My anger is for Tobit. So he lied to you?"

"He lied to us all," Cora said. And then she retold the story because she had to ease her pain for fear of what it would do to her if she didn't.

Eleanor listened patiently. After Cora had told her everything, her big sister refilled their teacups and pushed Cora's to her. "You can't quit."

Cora stared at Eleanor. She did feel better after telling her what had happened between her and Tobit. A tumble of emotions stayed with her, but she wasn't quite as numb. "I can't keep working with him, seeing him every day." Her voice caught in her throat. "I think I'm in love with him and I can't—I just can't do that to myself every day."

"So don't see him every day. But follow through with your commitment. You mentioned the other day that Tobit thought his doctor would release him for work after the first of the year. Stay on until Christmas. If you don't, you'll regret it later on down the road when you look back."

Cora stared into her tea. "It's not that I don't want to teach. I like it. I love it."

Eleanor grasped Cora's hand. "Then finish what you started." She was quiet for a moment before she went on. "Cora, I'm not defending what Tobit did. It was wrong. But I think we mustn't judge him too harshly. 'For with what judgment ye judge, ye shall be judged,'" she quoted from the book of Matthew. "You and I don't have children so it's hard to put ourselves in his place, but I can understand his pain and why he did what he did. His choice was wrong, but he needed to protect Elijah. He didn't want his son to feel the rejection he felt."

A tear trickled down Cora's cheeks. "But he let me think he was an unmarried man."

"I know." Eleanor's eyes grew misty. "But after hearing your praises for him for weeks—what a good father he is, how important his students are to him—I don't believe he intentionally meant to hurt you. It must be hard to live a lie like that day after day. Can you imagine how isolating it would be to live in a community but never be able to share your past? Can you imagine how lonely he's been?"

Cora sniffed. "You're defending him."

"I am *not*," Eleanor said. "I'm protecting you from yourself. Because you need to recover from this. You'll find love again and you'll marry, I know you will. But I don't want you to look back one day and feel guilty for how you responded to this trial. It's *oll recht* to be hurt and be angry, to be sad. It's even *oll recht* to feel sorry for yourself for a bit. But if you leave your students now, you'll regret it later. I know you and I know you will."

Cora took a deep breath. "You're right." She closed her eyes, suddenly feeling very tired. "I'll go back to school on Monday and we'll continue to prepare for the Christmas program, and I'll finish out the term." She opened her eyes. "I think I'll go to bed."

"*Goot* idea." Eleanor squeezed Cora's shoulder. "Things won't look as dismal in the morning light. They never do."

Cora rose, as did Eleanor. *"Danki,"* Cora murmured. Then she did something she hadn't done in a long time: she threw her arms around her sister. As she hugged her tightly, she released a prayer of thanks for the love of her family and for *Gott* to bless Tobit in his time of need.

## Chapter Ten

Keeping an eye out for the hired van he'd called for, Tobit sat on a bale of straw next to his chicken house and tossed shelled corn over the fence. The air was cold and the sky overcast, but it felt good to be out of the house doing something productive. The hens clucked and scratched and he found their sounds oddly comforting. Amid personal upheaval, knowing that some things in life never changed was consoling. Animals needed to be fed and watered and their stalls cleaned regardless of a caretaker's situation. Elijah had been doing a great job over the last weeks caring for their livestock, but Tobit missed the routine and physical activity.

He heard a car approach on the main road, but it passed by their house and he dug into the bag of corn kernels again. He had a doctor's appointment and if it went well, he'd receive a new plaster cast from below his knee to his ankle. The shorter cast would make it much easier for him to move around.

After the appointment, he intended to go to a bakery near the medical offices and buy a small cake or maybe some fancy cupcakes. It was Elijah's thirteenth birthday and he wanted to make it special, especially considering the conversation he needed to have with his son. Not tonight, though. This evening, Tobit was determined to make Elijah's birthday one to remember. They would have the boy's current favorite meal: corn dogs, oven-baked French fries and canned fruit cocktail. Then he would open the presents Tobit had already wrapped in brown paper. Most years, there was a single gift; the Amish didn't fuss over birthdays like Englishers did. This year, however, Tobit had purchased three gifts and spent far more money than usual. He told himself he hadn't overspent to compensate for the mess he had made of their lives, but he knew it was true.

Since Cora had left his house two days before, Tobit had thought of nothing *but* that mess. Thinking of the exchange with her that had precipitated her slamming his back door, he shivered and pulled his knit cap down farther on his head.

He didn't know what to do, about Cora or Aida. Was the solution to sell the house and move again? He shifted his gaze to his barnyard. The ten-acre property was nice with a neat, three-bedroom house and an adequate two-story barn and outbuildings. He liked it here. He liked the school where he taught and the Honeycomb community. He had taken to the people here and if he was honest with himself, he didn't want to leave. He had never done that in the middle of a school year; leaving the children or the men who hired him in the lurch that way wasn't right. But maybe no one would care. According to Elijah, the students loved Cora, as did the parents.

But he couldn't run from his past forever. Cora had made him see that, at last.

A sound in the lane drew Tobit's attention. It wasn't his ride. This was the clip-clopping of hoofbeats. He grabbed his crutches and slowly hoisted himself onto his good leg. It was Elden in his wagon. Tobit watched as his friend drove into the barnyard and secured his dapple gray to the hitching post.

"What are you doing here?" Tobit asked when Elden was close enough to hear him.

"*Goot* to see you, too," Elden responded, sliding his hands into his pockets. "I might ask you the same thing. Why are you out here? Far as I know, you're not supposed to be doing farm work on that leg yet."

Tobit shifted his weight on the crutches. The temperature had dropped since he came outside and dark clouds moved in the sky. Everyone said it was too early to snow in Delaware if it was going to snow at all this year, but it smelled like snow to him. "Waiting for my ride. I've got that doctor's appointment. Hoping to get this cast off and return home wearing trousers with two pant legs." He indicated the small canvas bag with the article of clothing he intended to take with him. "So what *are* you doing here?"

"I said I'd be back when I looked at your windmill after your accident. That part for the blade finally came in. Wind's not bad this morning so I thought I'd get you fixed up."

"I told you I don't want you up there. It's dangerous," Tobit grumbled. He appreciated that Elden wanted to help but after his own fall, he didn't feel he could ask anyone else to go up for him. It was still pumping water, and he planned to leave it until he could climb up there himself again.

"It won't be all that dangerous, thanks to my wife. Millie threw a fit when she found out I'd gone up to take a look. She made me buy a fancy harness from a mail-order catalog. You step into it, fasten it up and attach a line to the frame. According to her, if I fall, it will catch me and I'll be dangling off your windmill like a spider on a silk thread." Elden grinned.

Even though he didn't feel like it, Tobit managed a meager smile. His first urge was to protest again, but Elden and the extended Koffman family had been more than kind since his accident. It didn't seem right to get into an argument with his friend, who was trying to do the right thing. Had the roles been reversed and Elden had been the one in a cast, he'd do the same for him.

Tobit met Elden's steady gaze. "*Oll recht*, then, suit yourself. *Danki.*"

"*Gern gschehne,*" Elden responded politely with a nod.

But he didn't walk away to get to it. Instead, he stood there, head down, waiting until Tobit began to feel uncomfortable.

"Something else?" Tobit finally asked.

Elden scuffed his boot in the gravel and looked down. "Wondering if you want to talk."

Tobit shifted his gaze to the chickens strutting in their pen. "About what?"

"Not sure, my friend. But best I can tell, you've got something going on. You look as miserable as Cora. If I didn't know better, I'd think she'd been crying her eyes out for the last two days. It seemed like things were going well between you. You want to tell me what happened?"

Tobit groaned. He'd known this would happen. Once he told Cora about Aida, she'd tell her sisters and everyone in Honeycomb would know within a day. They'd make judgments and talk behind his back. "I'm sure she already told you," he responded coolly.

Elden shook his head slowly as if disappointed in Tobit. "Guess you don't know Cora as well as I thought you did. She's not one to gossip."

Tobit narrowed his gaze. "You're not telling me she didn't say anything to her sisters. Best I can tell, they share everything."

"I'd guess Millie and the others know, but no one's said a word to me, Jack or Felty. Not even my wife would discuss it with me. I suspect Cora thought whatever happened between the two of you, it's your story to tell."

Tobit stared past his friend at the dapple gray waiting patiently at the hitching rail. For some reason, hearing that Cora hadn't broadcast his business made him feel worse instead of better. Maybe unconsciously he'd hoped she would tell everyone so he didn't have to.

"Look, you don't have to tell me," Elden said, "but I've got a feeling you need to lighten your load." He hesitated. "I'm a good listener. Something my mother taught me." He cut his eyes at Tobit, his blue-gray eyes twinkling with amusement. "You know my *mam*. She likes to talk."

Tobit stood silent in indecision. He was inclined to keep his mouth shut. Even before Aida left, he hadn't been one of those people who liked to share his thoughts and feelings. It wasn't something done in his aunt and uncle's home. But at thirty-three, it was beginning to get old. And lonely. Cora had made him realize that, too.

With a sigh, he eased back onto the bale of straw. Once he started talking, the story poured out of him. He told his friend about Aida's leaving, how he and Elijah had bounced around from community to community, and why. He talked about Cora and how much he enjoyed the time he spent with her. How he'd found himself waiting each school day for her to stop by so they could grade papers together. He told Elden that he felt guilty for all of it and badly wished he'd done things differently ten years ago.

As Elden had assured, he was a good listener. He settled beside Tobit on the straw and listened, occasionally asking a question but never with judgment in his tone. When Tobit was done, he was exhausted but somehow felt better, as if someone else could now carry a portion of the load that was becoming too much for his shoulders.

"Phew," Elden muttered. "We say a prayer for you, Millie and I, every night when we have our family prayers. Now I wish we'd said two." He turned his gaze on Tobit. His face was solemn but lacked condemnation. "That's a heavy burden to bear. I wish you'd told me sooner."

"I'm sorry I lied to you," Tobit said despondently. He stared at the lane, wondering where his ride had gotten to. "I'm sorry I lied to Cora, to the school board members. To everyone in Honeycomb. But at the time, when the lie started after Aida left, you have to believe when I say I was doing it for Elijah. It was never for me."

Elden patted Tobit's knee. "I know you well enough

to believe that's true. You're not a selfish man." He crossed his arms thoughtfully. "You tell Elijah yet?"

"*Nay*. Today's his birthday. I want to have a nice dinner for him. I bought gifts. I won't have his thirteenth birthday ruined. I plan to tell him tomorrow. Or the next day," he added, dreading it.

"You need to tell him sooner than later. I would guess that all the Koffman girls know. Willa can be a gossip, even though she doesn't mean to be, and Jane's too young to know sometimes what should and shouldn't be said. Once someone lets it out, your situation will travel by Amish telegraph. Folks beyond Kent County will know in a week. You have to be the one to tell the boy his mother is still alive before someone at recess does. And you need to talk to one of our bishops. You must admit to your sin, Tobit, and ask for forgiveness. It's the only way to see any light at the end of this."

Tobit eyed him. "Cora said the same thing."

"Smart woman. But you already know that." Elden pointed at him. "You can see what the bishop advises once you've confessed. As I see it, you've got no choice but to find Aida and end this one way or the other. Either you and Aida need to start living as man and wife again or you should petition the church for the approval of a legal divorce. I know there aren't many divorces among us, but I imagine ten years of abandonment would be cause enough."

Tobit heard the sound of tires on the gravel driveway and looked up to see the white minivan he was expecting. Elden offered his arm to help him to his feet and after hesitating, he gripped it and stood.

"You know what the worst part of all of this is?" Tobit asked, accepting the crutches his friend handed him.

"What's that?"

Tobit shrugged, emotion tightening his chest. "I love her. I've fallen in love with Cora and I think she loves me." He looked away as his voice caught in his throat. "And I… I never thought I would ever have that."

Elden wiped his mouth with the back of his hand and glanced away. "Then I'm sorry for you and Cora both."

Two nights later, Tobit sat across the supper table from Elijah. When he'd gone to the doctor the other day, he'd stopped at Byler's on the way home. He'd picked up a few groceries, including the ingredients for the skillet lasagna Cora had described. Even using jarred tomato sauce, he was amazed by how good the simple dish was. His son must have agreed because he was presently wolfing down his third helping.

Tobit, who had barely eaten anything, pushed the cheesy pasta around on his plate. Even though it was delicious, he didn't have much appetite. Hadn't in days. "More?" he asked Elijah, reaching for the spoon resting in the frying pan in the center of the table.

"*Nay*, I'm good. Might heat some up and take it in a thermos to school in the morning. Charlie and I and a couple of the guys are building the stage for the Christmas program. Teacher says we have to do it outside, either rain or shine, cold or not, because she doesn't want a mess in the schoolhouse. It's not supposed to rain, but it's going to be near freezing. A hot meal for lunch will be good."

Tobit raised an eyebrow. He'd been turning over in

his mind for hours how he was going to broach the subject of the boy's mother and was relieved to have something else to talk about while he gathered his courage. "A stage?" he scoffed. "This isn't a Broadway show!"

Elijah took another piece of garlic bread from a baking sheet on the table. "I have no idea what that means, *Dat*."

"Doesn't matter." He looked at Elijah across the table from him and tapped the corner of his mouth. "Napkin."

Elijah took the paper towel beside his plate and wiped his face.

"What's the stage for?" Tobit asked, annoyed all over again that Cora had decided to do the Christmas program without asking him. It felt good to be upset with her; it made him miss her less. "You're not doing a nativity play with talking donkeys and sheep, are you? I doubt Bishop Cyrus would approve. Or any of the others in the county."

Elijah rolled his eyes. "There's no talking animals. Somebody is reading from the Bible about the baby's birth." He wrinkled his nose. "One of the girls. I don't know which one. Some of the littles will have a mini spelling bee and a couple of the older kids will read essays about Christmas and stuff."

"Don't need a stage for that," Tobit groused. "Students can stand in front of my desk. Cora's," he corrected.

"*Dat*, the stage is so the parents can see everyone when we all stand together to sing." Elijah spoke as if his father had said the most outlandish thing. "It's kind of like a wide staircase that doesn't go anywhere. Matty and Martha's *dat* donated the wood from his sawmill.

Teacher said it would be a good math lesson, with us having to measure and stuff."

"So it's a riser, not a stage?"

"Don't know what that means, either." Elijah took a big bite of bread and continued. "We'll stand on the stage—"

"Risers," Tobit corrected.

"Risers." Elijah nodded. "When we stand on them, our voices will carry into the room better. Teacher says we sound amazing already, but we'll be more amazing by Christmas Eve." He beamed. "She says my singing has improved. That you're going to be proud of me."

"Does she, now?" Tobit asked. His son had nothing but praise for Cora. It was obvious that he liked her, which pained him. She had been a good influence since she'd taken over the school, getting his son to take his lessons more seriously. She'd also given him gentle praise in ways that came more easily to women than men.

Elijah crammed the rest of the bread into his mouth. "Oh, and we're also making this wall thing that we'll put cork strips on so we can tack schoolwork on it. After Christmas, we can use it as a divider when Teacher puts us in groups. Teacher brought in rag rugs so we could—"

"Elijah, I need to talk to you about something," Tobit interrupted. He didn't want to hear any more about Cora's changes in the schoolhouse or how wonderful the program would be.

"*Oll recht.* Will it take long? I have reading to do after I wash up the dishes. Teacher says we have to read for at least half an hour every night."

Tobit drew his hand over his mouth. His heart pounded and even though he'd rehearsed what he would say to Elijah about his mother, the words escaped him now. All he could think was, what if his son hated him for what he'd done? What would he do then?

"It won't take long," Tobit said. "And if you have a lot of homework, I can wash the dishes."

"Should you be standing at the sink?"

"I'm supposed to be putting a little weight on it. The cast is made so I can stand for a few minutes at a time. Next time I go in, I'll get a walking cast if things still look good." He was stalling again.

Elijah nodded, taking a piece of crust to sop up some tomato sauce still on his plate. "What did you want to talk to me about?"

Tobit pushed his plate away to lean forward, his folded arms on the table. "I did something wrong a very long time ago. I'm not proud of it and tomorrow I'm going to talk to Bishop Cyrus and make amends with the church and *Gott*." He felt like he couldn't breathe but he pushed on. "But I need to tell you about it because soon everyone in Honeycomb will know."

Elijah suddenly looked apprehensive and met his father's gaze with pale blue eyes identical to Tobit's. With the boy's last growth spurt, he looked even more like his father than he had before. But Tobit prayed he wouldn't be like him. He wanted his son to be able to make better choices than he had, and he wanted him to know that he was loved, something Tobit had never felt.

"You're making me nervous, *Dat*. What is it? Are you sick? Are you going to die? Just tell me."

"No, I'm not sick. I'm not going anywhere." Tobit

squeezed the boy's hand. "It's about your mother, Elijah."

Elijah froze. "What?"

"She didn't die. I lied to you, *sohn*. I lied to everyone." Tobit's voice caught in his throat. "Your mother didn't die when you were a little boy. She left us."

Elijah squinted, dropping his last bit of bread onto his plate. "I don't understand."

"I don't either," Tobit admitted soberly. "But it's what happened."

In the next half an hour, Tobit explained to his son the details of his mother's disappearance when he was three. Tobit tried to be as honest as possible about what happened and how he felt about it. He took care, however, not to say anything bad about Aida because no matter what she had done, she was still his mother. He told the sequence of events and how he responded as simply as he could.

As Tobit spoke, Elijah's eyes welled with tears that tore at Tobit's heart. The whole reason he'd carried on this pretense for so many years was to protect his boy. Cora had said *Gott* could forgive him, but Tobit wondered if she could ever forgive him. And could he forgive himself?

When Tobit had said all he wanted to say, at least for the time being, he fell silent. He sipped his water and looked back at his son again. "Do you have any questions?"

Elijah used his fist to wipe at his eyes. "Do…do you know where she is now?"

"I don't." Tobit's heart had slowed to a normal pace and he had better control of his emotions. He still felt terrible for committing the same sin repeatedly, but he also felt relief for having told his son the truth.

"Do...do you think my *mam* has been looking for us?" Elijah pressed.

Tobit hesitated before answering. Should he be truthful with his son, or had there been enough total honesty for one day? His gut feeling was that Aida had not looked for them. That she had walked off their little farm and never looked back. But he could see their son was already hurting and didn't want to make him feel worse. "I... I don't know, Elijah." And that was the truth, one that hadn't crossed his mind in many years.

"Are you...are you going to try to find her?"

"I don't know that, either. I plan to talk to Bishop Cyrus tomorrow. It's my hope that he'll advise me. Tell me what I need to do to make this right." Tobit studied his son, trying to gauge what the boy wanted. "Do you want me to try to find her?"

Elijah set his fork and knife on his plate, wiped his mouth with the paper towel again, crumpled it and set it in the middle of the plate. "I don't know if I want to know where she is. If I want to see her or not."

"Fair enough," Tobit said, surprised at how well his son was taking the news.

Elijah got up from his chair and picked up his dirty plate. He didn't look at Tobit when he spoke. "You know, in a way, it was better to think about her as dead and gone to heaven than to think about her living somewhere else. Not caring about me."

Tobit wanted to argue that of course his mother cared about him. He wanted to say Aida loved him, but he didn't know that to be true. She had never bonded with him or seemed to take pleasure in him, not even when he was an infant. At the time, he'd told himself that she would learn to be a good mother and love Elijah, but that had not happened. And Elijah had never been comfortable with her, either. When he fell and scraped his knee learning to walk, it was his father he had wanted. It had been the same when the boy had been sick in the middle of the night. It was Tobit who had walked him, not Aida.

"I guess I've felt the same way all this time," Tobit admitted, rising. "Even though I knew she was still alive, I pretended she wasn't because it was easier."

Elijah carried his plate to the sink and set it on the counter. "If it's *oll recht* with you, I think I'll go upstairs and do my reading." His back was still to his father. "And leave you to the dishes."

Tobit used the table for support to make his way around it without his crutches. A part of him wanted to hug the boy, but it wasn't something he'd done in a long time and he didn't want to upset him. "That's fine. There's not much here." He hesitated, and then, balancing on his good foot, he rested his hand on Elijah's shoulder. "I want you to know how sorry I am. For all of this."

"I know." Elijah turned around at last. He wasn't near Tobit's height of over six feet yet, but he'd grown since they arrived in Honeycomb.

"Is there anything else you want to ask me?" Tobit said.

Elijah exhaled. "*Nay*, not now. But if I have a question about her, can I ask later? Or will it make you angry?"

Another piece of Tobit's heart crumbled. "Of course you can ask me. And I promise I'll try not to get annoyed, but if I do, you remind me that I said I wouldn't, okay?"

Elijah nodded. "I'm going to go do my homework now."

Tobit watched as the teen crossed the kitchen.

When the boy reached the doorway, he turned back. "Can I tell Charlie about my *mam*?"

"You can. But you'll have to decide who you want to tell and who you don't. At least for now. And, of course, once I confess to the bishop, word's going to get out. There are some who will judge her. Certainly, judge me. You need to be ready for that."

"But *Dat*, you were just trying to protect me."

This time it was Tobit who teared up. "Ya, I was." He swallowed hard. "Did you say you had reading to do?"

Elijah walked out of the kitchen, leaving Tobit with the dirty dishes and his thoughts.

## Chapter Eleven

Cora glanced up from her desk and the math test she was grading. Two of her third graders hadn't yet completed theirs, so the other children read silently while waiting for their classmates to finish. She had put all the third graders at a block of desks directly in front of hers. Tobit had arranged the desks in rows the same way they had been when Cora went to the Clover school. However, she'd read an article at the public library about pushing desks together in groups and decided to try it. So far, it was working well.

While the third graders took their test, her sixth and above were working on essays at two large wooden tables she'd rescued from alongside the road. With the stools they already had, the tables worked well for all sorts of activities like science projects and group work. The first and second graders were in the coatroom, where two older girls read to them and asked questions Cora had provided. Her fourth and fifth graders were seated on the floor near the woodstove, cutting up old Christmas cards to make new ones. As she counted her chicks, she reminded herself that Charlie, Elijah and the troublemaking cousins, Johnny and Noah, were outside working on the risers they were building for the Christmas program. Once the rest of the math tests were turned in, she'd go out and check on the boys to be sure they weren't out there goofing around.

Cora smiled as she looked down at the test in front of her. To someone who had never attended a one-room schoolhouse, the space might seem like chaos, but these days, she felt like she was getting the hang of teaching multiple grades at once. She liked to think that it was *organized* chaos. She used Tobit's curriculum based on the state's education requirements, but she followed her instincts in how she taught. That wasn't to say that she thought his techniques were bad, but she'd found ways to teach that worked better for her. For one thing, she'd discovered that switching tasks regularly with all the age groups resulted in keeping her students' attention longer. That and giving them more but shorter breaks for lunch and recess allowed her to get through more lessons than previously.

The sound of a thin, sweet voice drew Cora's attention and she looked up, trying to figure out where it was coming from. She couldn't tell if it was a boy or a girl.

"Silent night, holy light. All is gone, all is bright."

Cora rose from her creaky wooden chair to get a better look.

"Rounded versions, mother and child," the voice continued.

Cora smiled to herself at the error in the lyrics. She had a good idea who the soloist was. As she walked around the third graders' desks, she sang to herself, "Holy infant, so tender and mild."

"Teacher?" A small hand touched hers. "Can I ask a question?" Amos Chubb, a third grader, asked, keeping his voice down.

Cora stopped. "You may, but you best hurry and finish up your test." She glanced at a clock on the wall to the right of the new whiteboard. At the beginning of the term, Tobit had requested the school board buy the *newfangled* item. The older men had dragged their feet, insisting the twenty-plus-year-old chalkboard was good enough. His response had been to buy one with his own money and install it himself.

Realizing an hour hadn't yet passed since the last time she thought about Tobit, she groaned. She didn't want to think about him. He was another woman's husband. It was wrong to dwell on thoughts of him, but it was hard not to. She missed him and the short-lived dream that he might be the man *Gott* intended to be her husband. The idea that she couldn't get Tobit out of her head made her angry. But her anger was easier to deal with than the pain of her bruised, if not broken, heart. She continually told herself that she hadn't been in love with him; she hadn't known him long enough to have those feelings. It hadn't helped much.

Amos peered up at Cora expectedly and she realized he was still waiting. All week it had been like this. Her attention span was shorter than her students'. She crouched at his desk until they were eye to eye. She still faintly heard the words to "Silent Night" coming from the back of the room. "What's your question?"

He chewed on the eraser of his #2 pencil and peered

at her through thick wire-frame glasses. "Why would someone eat eighteen eggs?"

"What?"

Amos pointed at the final math question on his test. It was a word problem: If Mary had three dozen eggs and used eighteen for breakfast, how many would she have left?

Cora smiled at him. "She didn't eat them. She scrambled them for her family." She widened her eyes. "Or maybe she made an omelet with sausage and cheese inside."

He frowned. "But it don't say she made scrambled eggs for everyone."

"*Nay*, it *doesn't*," she agreed, using the right form of the verb rather than correcting him. She found it more effective long term. "But you can guess that's what she might have done with all those eggs. It doesn't matter what she did with them. Solve the problem and show your work." She stood. "You know how many are in a dozen, right, Amos?"

He smirked at her as if that was the silliest thing he'd ever been asked. He lowered his head and began to write out the numbers to work the problem.

"Silent night, holy night," came the unknown soloist's voice. The chorus was louder.

Cora made her way past the group's desks and tables and found the source of the singing. It was coming from an unoccupied desk. The seat was empty. She stooped and looked beneath the desk. Sure enough, there was Apple Detweiler. While the girl was technically a third grader, she wasn't required to take the math test due to her intellectual limitations. "Apple, what are you doing under here? I thought you were making Christmas cards."

"I wanted to practice for the Christmas party," Apple told her, and then she sang, "Sheep herds quake at the sight."

Cora offered her hand, smiling. "Come on. Let's see how the others are doing with their Christmas cards."

Apple, who had chubby round cheeks and bright blue eyes, beamed at Cora. As Cora led her to the group of students on the floor on the far side of the room, she took solace in the feel of Apple's hand in hers. She had been so devastated by Tobit's confession. She had left his home feeling lost and hopeless. But the warmth of Apple's small hand reminded her of all the good in the world, all the joy still there, even amid the sadness Cora feared would never subside.

As Cora handed Apple a piece of red construction paper, the coatroom door flew open with a bang and a whoosh of cold air. "Teacher! Teacher! Look who's here," Noah Mast announced, bursting into the main room of the schoolhouse. "We have a visitor!"

Cora released Apple's hand as the little girl slid down to sit next to one of her sisters. "A visitor? Who—" Before the words were out of her mouth, a tall, broad-shouldered man filled the doorway.

For an instant, Cora thought she was seeing things. How could Tobit be there? He couldn't get into his buggy on his own and certainly couldn't have walked there. Had he gotten a ride? "Tobit," she said, hoping her voice didn't quaver.

His unflinching gaze met hers. "Cora," he said.

Noah Mast looked from one of his teachers to the other as if trying to figure out what was happening.

Cora hoped her face didn't reveal her shock at seeing Tobit for the first time since their breakup from the courtship that never began. She hoped the children couldn't see her yearning for what would never be.

"I… I apologize for barging in like this in the middle of the school day." Tobit sounded as uneasy as she felt. "But… Someone dropped off some greenery— pine boughs, cedar, holly—and I thought your students might want to use them to decorate for the Christmas program. Elijah and the other boys are putting it in the woodshed. I wouldn't bring it inside for another week so that it will last until Christmas."

"Someone dropped them off?" Cora asked.

"Sorry. I don't know his name. One of the older men who play checkers outside of Raber's." His forehead wrinkled the way it did when he was unsure of something. "Zook's the surname."

"Was it Amos or Bert?" she asked, though it didn't matter. She didn't care who brought the greenery. She only wanted to continue the conversation with Tobit. She missed him so much.

"I'm not sure," he answered, still standing in the doorway between the cloakroom and the schoolroom as if he feared he wouldn't be welcome in his own school. "They're interchangeable, aren't they?"

Somehow she managed a smile, even though she was still angry with him. "They do look nearly identical," she agreed. "And Amos is only ten months older than Bert. Born the same year." She didn't know why she was babbling on about the Zooks.

"Teacher!" Spotting Tobit, Apple Detweiler jumped up from the floor and raced toward him.

Cora cringed, calling out to her student not to run, but it was too late.

Apple was tall for her age and round, and for a moment, Cora feared she would knock Tobit over. As Apple flung herself against him, hugging him, Tobit managed to grasp the doorjamb and steady himself.

Cora saw now that he was wearing long pants for the first time in many weeks and her gaze went to his bare toes sticking out from a new black cast. She'd forgotten that Elden said Tobit's doctor's appointment had gone well and that he'd been fitted with a new cast. According to her brother-in-law, he was permitted to walk on it for short periods without his crutches.

"Apple," Tobit said, sounding genuinely pleased to see her. The little girl wrapped her arms around her teacher, and he hugged her back.

Then all the students were out of their chairs, surrounding him in greeting, all talking at once. A girl showed him the Christmas card she had made while a boy told him about the baseball game they'd played at recess the day before. And even the older students were there, giggling and talking about how the Christmas program would be the best ever.

Cora stood back from the fray and observed. At the beginning of the school year, Charlie had insisted the students didn't like Tobit. He said the new teacher was mean. The children, all talking at once and eager to see him, didn't seem to agree with Charlie. She smiled, her happiness bittersweet. She was glad for Tobit that the children missed him; it would make it easier after the first of the year when he returned. But she was sad for herself because she already knew what a wonderful person he was and that he would never be hers.

The other boys who had been working outside burst in with another draft of icy December air and the schoolroom got even louder. Cora walked back toward the front of the classroom, picking up Amos Chubb's completed math test as she went by his desk. As she settled into her chair to finish grading the papers, one of the older girls, fourteen-year-old Martha Yost, approached Cora's desk.

"Teacher?"

*"Ya?"*

Martha plucked at the skirt of her pale green dress, not making eye contact. She was a good student and always helpful with the younger children, but she was shy and struggled to make friends. "D…do you think— I… I wondered if—" She fell silent and looked as if she was about to walk away without saying what she came to say.

"What is it, Martha?" Cora asked gently.

"I know… I know we're not supposed to have rehearsal until after lunch, but…but… Do you think we could practice the Christmas hymns for the program now? So Teacher can hear us? Because he said he wanted to." Martha's words came out in a rush that seemed to surprise her as much as Cora.

Cora thought for a moment. She tried to stick to her daily schedule, but what harm would it do to switch the day around a bit? It might be good for the students to sing in front of someone other than her. "I think that would be *oll recht*, Martha," she answered. "But I have papers to grade, so if you want us to have rehearsal this morning, you'll have to run it."

Martha's dark brown eyes got as round as tea saucers. "I… I can't… I don't…"

"You don't what?" Cora asked. "You know all the songs by heart, every verse, and you know the order they're to be sung in. And you're the one I depend on to start on the right note and keep up the tempo."

The girl pressed long, slender fingers to the top of the battered walnut desk. "But I don't know how to run a rehearsal," she murmured anxiously.

Cora tapped her red grading pen on her desk. "It's easy enough. Gather the students at the west wall where we've been practicing. Have them stand in their assigned places and start the first song. Everyone is singing that one. Then go to the next."

"D-do we have to do the other parts? Like…like read the verse from the Bible?"

"*Nay.* We should save something for Christmas Eve for Teacher, shouldn't we?" Cora smiled at her.

Martha clasped her hands together. "He wants to hear us," she said again. "I can do this."

"You can do this," Cora agreed. Then she leaned forward and lowered her voice. "I'll tell you a trick to doing things that challenge your comfort. I was so nervous when I started teaching here that I used it."

"You were nervous?" Martha breathed in awe.

"Of course I was. I've never taught before. But do you know what? I did what my *mam* used to tell my sisters and me when we were uneasy doing something new. I pretended I wasn't afraid. I pretended I knew what I was doing, and you know what, Martha? It worked.

Eventually, I wasn't afraid or even nervous anymore. I found my confidence in doing the thing that scared me."

Martha looked down at Cora. *"Danki."*

*"Gern gschehne,"* Cora replied and returned to her task.

The children rehearsed for the next three-quarters of an hour while Tobit sat on a stool in front of them. Cora tried to take advantage of the unexpected free time and grade papers while the children sang, but she found it hard to concentrate. She kept looking up from her desk at Tobit. Thankfully he was seated with his back to her so he didn't know. She had forgotten what a big man he was. Once she had gotten to know him and he wasn't scary anymore, it hadn't seemed to matter. He was at least six feet tall, and his shoulders were broad, his hands twice the size of hers. He looked thinner than when she had last seen him and his hair looked shaggy.

She had once imagined what it would be like to cut his hair for him, for her husband. Even though she had never touched it, she knew it would be soft and smooth between her fingertips. Such an intimate task would mean she would be close enough to feel the warmth of his body and smell the shampoo in his hair.

Catching her thoughts running away from her again, she gulped and circled another misspelling on a rough draft she was reading. As she finished poring over the essay and went on to another, she heard the last notes of the final song and the children scattered. She glanced at the clock behind her; it was nearly lunchtime.

Cora heard Tobit walking toward her before she looked up to see him. He carried his coat over his arm and slowly limped across the room.

When he reached her desk, she asked, "Walking cast?"

"*Ya.* The doctor says I'm doing well. I see him again in ten days, but he thinks I can be out of a cast the first of January if I continue to heal well."

She forced a smile. He looked tired and she saw sadness in his blue eyes. "That's good to hear." She looked past him. "Time to tidy up your workspaces, and then I want everyone in their chairs for daily journal entries," she said loudly to be heard above the din.

Several of the students groaned.

She looked at Tobit. He seemed to want to say something, but what was there to say? A lump rose in her throat. She wished he'd go before he made her cry in front of the children.

"Cora, can I talk to you?" he asked, lowering his voice so no one else could hear him.

She considered telling him he'd taken up enough of her time in the middle of the school day and sending him on his way. But she couldn't bring herself to speak the words.

"Privately," he murmured.

She met his blue eyes and was helpless to look away for a moment. Then she stood. "I'm going to walk Teacher out," she announced. "Charlie and Elijah, could you stoke the woodstove and add some more wood? It's getting cool in here. Everyone else, you know what I expect from you."

Cora let Tobit lead the way and when they were in the coatroom, she closed the door so the students couldn't hear them. She faced him with arms crossed and waited.

Now he seemed nervous. "I… I wanted to tell you

that I took your advice. I spent time with your uncle last week. With Bishop Cyrus. He…he was kind. We talked about me making a confession before the church, which I agreed to. I um…asked to be a part of his congregation."

Cora pressed her lips together, thinking that as members of the same congregation, they would see each other on Sundays, every other week. A part of her was gladdened by the thought of it, but she wondered if it would be easier not to see him at all. Of course, they lived in a small, tight-knit community, so avoiding each other completely would be impossible.

"I've never had to confess publicly before. But then at least everyone will know and the ruse will finally be over." He met her gaze. *"Ya?"*

*"Ya,"* she echoed. She knew it would be hard for him, but it was the way of their church. He would stand before the congregation and admit to the sin or sins he had committed. He would vow to be a better man and then be granted forgiveness as only *Gott* could do. "It's the right thing to do. And you'll feel better once it's done." As she spoke, she felt her anger slip away. The tone of his voice made her realize how repentant he was for what he had done and she knew that she, too, could forgive him. With time and prayer.

"Bishop Cyrus insists I need to find Aida." He shifted his weight as if he was uncomfortable standing on his injured leg.

"And then what?" Cora blurted with no forgiveness in her tone.

Tobit's eyes crinkled at the edges, and she felt bad that she had said it.

"The bishop says we have to live as a family or… divorce."

Cora had never known someone Amish who was divorced. Divorce was a drastic measure in their church. It was almost unheard of and reserved for only the most severe cases: extended criminal behavior or severe physical abuse.

Not sure what to say, she nodded.

"I talked to Elijah. About his mother," Tobit continued.

"He knows?" she asked with surprise. She'd seen no changes in his behavior since she'd stopped going to his house except that he'd asked her the previous week if she was all right.

Tobit stroked his short-cropped beard. "I told him last week."

"And how did he…how is he taking the news?"

Tobit thought for a moment before he answered. "Surprisingly well. He understood why I did it. He's not happy with me, but he's not angry, either. Disappointed, maybe?"

The cloakroom door opened. It was Mary Emily Chubb, one of Amos's older sisters. "Sorry. Matty picked that scab on his hand again. Can I get a Band-Aid for him from your desk?"

Cora was suddenly aware of how small the cloakroom was and how close she and Tobit were standing. "*Ya*, of course. Once everyone's done their journal entries, they can get their lunch boxes." She indicated two long, neat rows of bags and pails on shelves. "We'll eat inside. I'm going to walk Teacher out and then I'll be in directly."

Mary Emily nodded and closed the door.

"I should go," Tobit said. But he didn't move. "I have to say, Cora, I knew you were a good teacher, but seeing you with the students, you... You're an excellent teacher. And the children clearly like you. I'm glad you're here with them."

Cora knew it was wrong to be prideful, but she couldn't help feeling pleased by his compliment. "*Danki.* You know, after last week, I also quit."

He drew back. "Quit? Why?"

*How could he not know?* She looked down at the hardwood floor. "So I wouldn't have to see you anymore. Grading papers and such. I was afraid it would... hurt too much," she said, surprised she would admit such a thing to him.

"Oh, Cora. I know I said this before, but I am so sorry." His voice was full of emotion. "I feel terrible that I put us in the situation we found ourselves in."

He didn't have to explain what he meant. She knew he referred to their attraction to each other.

"I know," she answered.

Then they were quiet for a few moments, surrounded by jackets, hats and lunch bags. The coatroom smelled faintly of wool and pine floor cleaner.

"I should go," he said.

"How did you even get here?" she asked, following him to the door.

He opened it, stepped out onto the landing and gestured. Elijah's Shetland pony and cart were tied to the hitching post.

Cora grinned. "You came in your son's *pony* cart?"

He shrugged as he slipped into his coat. "It was the

only way I could think to get here. I can't walk the distance, even though it's only half a mile, and I knew better than to try and hitch my wagon or buggy. Too high to climb into on my own."

She watched as he slowly went down the three steps to the ground, leaning on the rail. "Do you want Elijah to take you home?"

"*Nay*, I'll be fine."

Though it was cold and she was without her cloak, she watched him from the doorway as he crossed the yard, unhitched the pony and got into the cart. Because it was child-sized and he was so tall, he didn't have to step up. He simply slid onto the bench seat. When he guided the pony into the lane and stopped near the steps, Cora had to cover her mouth to keep from giggling aloud. "You look—" She sniggered. "You're so big and the cart's so small that you look like you're wearing it," she teased.

He glanced around him. The bench he sat on wasn't much wider than he was. "I suppose I do look foolish." He looked up at her. "But I'm glad I came. I wasn't sure how you would feel about me being here. I was afraid you might kick me out or something."

"I'm glad you came, too," she admitted.

As he lifted the reins, he smiled at her and Cora had to turn away to hide the tears that welled in her eyes. If she'd had any doubts before that she loved him, she had them no longer. And as she walked back into the school, closing the door behind her, she prayed that someday *Gott* would relieve her of the ache in her heart.

## Chapter Twelve

On a Saturday morning, Tobit sat on a wooden stool in Ezra Amsbary's parlor and taped up a box of bed linens. He had never met Ezra and never would. The elderly widower had moved to Ohio to live with his son and his family before Tobit and Elijah arrived in Honeycomb in August. The box sealed, he used a thick marker to write the contents on the lid and slid it off to the side.

The house was filled with the sounds of footsteps, laughter and voices. While men moved furniture and carried boxes to a waiting van, women packed up the kitchen. The house smelled of pine cleaner and the cinnamon rolls one of the women had put into the oven to be served when everyone took a coffee break later. All of Ezra's belongings would be shipped to his new home, where he'd live in a *dawdi haus* his son had built on his property.

Tobit was in a bad mood and didn't want to be there. He didn't want to be surrounded by all these cheerful, helpful people when he was so miserable. He had come only because Bishop Cyrus had invited him to join the

Saturday community service and refused to take no for an answer. When counseling Tobit, the bishop made it clear that Tobit must change the person he had become to protect his lies. That meant being more open to friendship and community and joining in activities. It wasn't that Tobit disagreed, but today wasn't the day to turn over a new leaf. He was fretful and worried and would have preferred to stay home to stew alone in his bad humor.

But it wasn't volunteering to give up a morning to pack boxes that had him upset. It was the call he'd made the day before to Aida's cousin whom he'd tracked down in Lancaster, Pennsylvania. He'd made the call on impulse, remembering that Aida had talked about visiting her cousin whose husband owned a popcorn store. The only reason he remembered Mary and John, whom he had never met, was because they had an unusual surname and he'd never heard of a popcorn store, so it stuck with him. He had found them with a single call to Nissley's Popcorn, the only place that featured the snack in the town. Tobit had talked to both John and Mary, and they had been more than kind, but the conversation had been brief and disturbing. They had been unwilling to give him any information about Aida but instead suggested he visit her elderly parents, who had recently moved to Millersville in Lancaster County. Tobit didn't want to talk to Peter and Rhoda Moller. But he knew he had to. Now that he had told his son what he had done, he had to make it right. Or at least make it as right as possible at this point.

A loud thud in the hallway outside the parlor brought Tobit to his feet. He moved as quickly as possible to the doorway to find Elden setting a large box down. In front of him was a smaller box lying upside down on the floor.

"I hope that wasn't full of glasses," Tobit quipped as he limped into the hall and leaned over to retrieve the box.

"Hey, I can get that," Elden said.

The top of the box had ripped free in the fall, so Tobit rolled it right side up. "I know you can, but if you pick up the bigger one, I can set this one on top for you. Easier on your back."

"You're not supposed to be on your feet. You told me your toes were swollen last night because you did too much. Where are your crutches?"

Tobit pointed to the parlor.

Elden scowled. "You're not going to be happy until you're back in the hospital, are you." It was a statement, not a question. He glanced at the box. "Looks like I'm going to need some more tape."

"I've got plenty." Tobit limped back into the parlor, which was empty except for the boxes that had been brought to him to be taped and labeled.

Elden followed him.

Tobit grabbed a roll of tape but dropped it and it rolled out of his reach. He groaned. "I can't do anything right today," he muttered. "I mismarked two boxes already. Dropped one on the good foot and gave myself a paper cut that might need to be stitched. I got blood on a perfectly good box."

Elden half smiled. "How you doing?" he asked quietly as he retrieved the tape.

Tobit sat down on the stool again. After the call to Aida's cousin, he'd taken the pony cart to Elden's to tell him he'd found her. Well, not found his wife, but her family. They'd know where she was. "Doing *oll recht*."

"You make up your mind about seeing the parents?" Elden sat across from him on a cardboard box labeled GLOVES, HATS, SCARVES.

"It's not like I have a choice, is it?"

Elden hesitated and then shook his head. *"Nay."*

"What if she's living with her parents or near them?" Tobit asked, not bothering to whisper. The entire Koffman family knew about Aida now, as did several other folks in Honeycomb. It was only a matter of time until everyone knew, and as he had told Cora at the school, he didn't care. "Maybe that's why John and Mary didn't want to tell me anything about her." He absently rubbed his leg, which was sore from walking after being in bed for weeks. "What if she's married to someone else? Married to someone who's made her happy, something I could never do?"

"I think you need to find her without dwelling on all the possibilities. You won't know how to deal with the situation until you know what the situation is."

"You're right. I know you're right." Tobit glanced out the window into a bare winter pasture that no longer held livestock. "I talked to Elijah about going with me to Millersville. He says he won't go. He's afraid she might be there and doesn't want to meet her." He turned back to Elden. "How am I supposed to fix this if our son doesn't want to see her?" He frowned. "I even tried to bribe him with the idea of missing two days of school. One day to go and come back, the next day to rest after the trip."

"Didn't work?" Elden asked.

Tobit shook his head. "How about you? Would you go with me? I hired a van for Monday."

Elden folded his hand. "*Ya*, if you want me to. Of course I'll go. But, um, do you mind if Millie comes? It might be helpful to have a woman with us. Since we don't know what you'll find."

"Of course Millie can come. I can use all the support I can get." He slid an open box closer, wondering how long he had to stay at Ezra's. He and Elijah had come in the pony cart, and the boy was outside with Charlie cleaning up the barn in preparation for the sale of the property. His son wouldn't want to go home before Charlie did.

"Guess I best get back to carrying boxes," Elden said, coming to his feet. "I'll only need this for a sec." He held up the roll of packing tape.

"There you are!"

The sound of Cora's voice drew Tobit's attention at once. She was looking at Elden. "Millie needs you in the kitchen. Something about the pantry shelves."

"On it." Elden slipped by her, set the tape on the boxes in the hall and disappeared.

Cora remained in the doorway but didn't speak. Tobit struggled to come up with something to say to her. He missed her visits to grade papers. Falling from his windmill had been worth the time he'd spent with her and he wished he could relive those hours. And the hour he had spent at the school the other day had been something he would remember always. The children had made him feel like he was really making a difference in their lives by being their teacher.

"*Goot* to see you getting out," she said. She wore a

blue tab dress and a white apron smudged with dirt. Instead of a prayer *kapp*, her hair was covered with a navy blue headscarf, tied at the nape of her neck. He could see wisps of red hair.

Tobit picked up another roll of tape and began to close the box in front of him to give him something to do with his hands. "It was your uncle's idea. He says I need to do community service. That it will be good for my soul," he groused.

"Sounds reasonable to me." She offered a hesitant smile. "Elden told me you found some of your wife's family."

Tobit's head popped up. "He did?"

*"Ya."*

"So everyone is talking about me?" He sighed. "Foolish question. Of course they are." He noticed that his finger had begun to bleed again and wiped it on his pant leg. "I'm going to visit her parents next week. This side of Lancaster. Monday. I was planning to take Elijah out of school."

"Of course," she said, moving into the room. "I'll miss him, but I understand."

"I meant I was *planning* to do it, but there's no need because he says he doesn't want to go. He's afraid she'll be there and he doesn't want to meet her. Not yet, at least, he says." He stared at the box. "Do you think I should make him go?"

She paused, then took a step closer to him. "You want my opinion?"

"I do." He continued to avoid eye contact with her. "You know him pretty well. And…and I respect your opinion."

"Well…" She exhaled. "He's afraid of the unknown. Like all of us. But he's still a boy, Tobit. Even though he's thirteen and able to do men's work, he's still a child. If he were my son," she continued thoughtfully, "I think I would go without him. Find his *mudder* first. Get an idea of the situation. That way, you can… The two of you," she corrected, "can figure out the best way to handle your next steps. If you and your wife have a plan, I think that will make things easier for Elijah."

He smiled sadly. "You're a good friend, Cora." He rubbed a finger along the paper cut on his hand. "Would you go with us? With me and Elden and Millie? It's Monday. I already hired a van." As soon as the words were out of his mouth, he regretted them. After what he had done to her, how could he ask such of thing of her?

"Would I go with you to meet *your wife*?" she asked incredulously.

He swallowed. Wrong or not, the idea of having her with them made the trip feel more manageable. "I know I shouldn't ask, but you're a good friend, and you and Elden are the only friends I have. I have no idea what's going to happen when I get to Millersville and I… I could use your support."

"I'd have to cancel school."

"*Ya*, but the children would love you all the more for it, wouldn't they?" He realized that his attempt to make light of the subject didn't work when she said nothing. "Could you at least think about it?" he asked, hoping he didn't sound too pathetic.

She walked out of the room without looking back. "*Ya*. I'll think about it."

\* \* \*

"Tobit wants you to do what?" Willa demanded loudly from the back of the buggy.

"Willa," Eleanor, who sat across from her and their father, admonished. She pointed to their father, who sat back, his mouth open, sound asleep.

"He's fine. Look, he didn't even move," Willa responded as she lowered her voice appropriately. "You're not considering going, are you?" she asked Cora.

Seated between Henry and Millie on the front bench seat, Cora turned to look over her shoulder at her sister. It was late afternoon, and they'd worked all day at the widower's house to pack up his belongings and ready the house for sale. Cora was tired, but working at the school, five days a week, she wasn't getting much physical activity. It felt good to have tired muscles and it had been nice to spend a day surrounded by friends and family.

While there had certainly been talk of the widower schoolteacher who was not actually a widower in Ezra Amsbary's kitchen, Cora had been pleasantly surprised by the kindness the women extended to Tobit. They had wondered aloud what could have made a woman leave her child and husband like that and had shown compassion for the situation. If anyone had any idea of the attraction Cora had felt for Tobit before learning that he was a married man, they hadn't spoken of it. Thankfully, while her sisters had known, they hadn't discussed it with anyone outside their family.

"He did ask me to go with him. Him and Elden and Millie," Cora added quickly.

"*Ya*, Elden told me at lunchtime," Millie said. "A

driver will pick Tobit up at seven thirty and they'll come to the store for us straight after. Even stopping for a big breakfast, we'll be at the in-laws' by noon."

"Cora, you can't go," Willa insisted, sliding across the bench seat that ran perpendicular to the front seat to be closer to her. "After what he did to you, leading you on to think he was single, you should never speak to him again."

"But what if no one knows where the wife is? If no one's seen her in all these years? Or she married some Englisher?" Jane argued. "You said that Tobit said she left her *kapp* behind. Even if he finds her, he can't be married to an Englisher. He wouldn't leave the church to be with a woman who left him and his child ten years ago!"

"There are plenty of single men out there without having to get tangled in that mess," Willa argued. She of all the Koffman sisters had dated the most and was therefore considered the expert on the matter in their house. "Sure, after all this time, she's not coming back to him, but how long will it take for him to get a legal divorce, and then the church has to approve it."

"I don't think it would be a problem for the church," Eleanor said. "She left him and she's been gone a very long time. And if she is an Englisher, which it's likely she is, the church would approve a divorce for that reason, as well."

Cora had tried not to dwell too much on what would happen if the marriage between Tobit and Aida was dissolved—for whatever reason. To hope for that seemed wrong, yet if he divorced because of what his wife had done, he would be free to marry her. When he'd first told her about Aida, she'd been too angry to consider the likely possibility of him soon being a divorced man. She was too upset that he had lied to her, but now after some time had passed, and her anger had subsided, the hope was rising in her chest again.

"How would you go if you wanted to?" Willa asked, still obviously against the idea. "You have to teach."

"I didn't say I was going," Cora answered. When Tobit had asked her that morning if she would accompany him to Pennsylvania, she'd had no intention of doing so. But later it occurred to her that maybe he was searching for Aida so that he could end the marriage. All this time he'd never attempted to do so, but was he doing it now so he could be with her? The fact that he hadn't said that didn't matter. He was too moral a man to say such a thing out loud.

Her gaze settled on her oldest sister. Eleanor had been so good to her the night she learned of Tobit's deception. But since then, she'd said very little on the subject, which was so like her. And like their mother. *Mam* had never taken sides. "What do you think I should do, Ellie? Go with them or not?"

Eleanor stared straight ahead in thought. She looked tired. Her friend Sara had been hospitalized again and Eleanor had been helping when she could. She had been taking meals over for the family and watching the children so Sara's husband could be at her bedside. The prognosis didn't look good. Each night during family devotions, the Koffmans prayed for Sara and her family.

"I think," Eleanor said slowly, "that you have to do what your heart tells you. I understand wanting to help Tobit get through this, but there's a remote possibility he might bring home his wife. So…" She drew out the word. "I think you should do what's best for you. You must care for your spirit. If you don't want to go, don't. But if you feel that going will help you, there's nothing wrong with that."

Cora faced forward again. As the sisters' conversation turned to what they talked most about these days—the store—she listened to the rhythmic sounds of their horse's hooves and the scrape, scrape, scrape of the wood and metal buggy wheels on the pavement. The sky had turned dark and it looked like it was about to rain. Or snow. The forecasts had been mixed.

As she watched the Amish farms and Englisher houses go by, she thought about what Eleanor had said. Her sister suggested that Cora had to do what was best for herself and not necessarily Tobit. Cora understood what she meant, but she still didn't know whether she should go or not.

She crossed her arms and leaned back in the leather seat. A pitter-patter began to sound on the roof of the buggy. At first, she thought it was rain, but then she saw the little clear balls bouncing off the windshield. Sleet. Her students were all talking about their hopes for snow for Christmas and in the days following when they would be on break.

In her current mood, the dark sky, and the sleet, seemed appropriate. *Nay,* she thought. *I won't go. It's time.* Her choice made, she waited for the relief, or maybe the satisfaction the decision would bring her. But it didn't. Instead, she was once again on the brink of tears.

# Chapter Thirteen

Like on any school day, Monday morning Cora woke at five thirty to the sound of her alarm. Still in her nightgown, she sank to her knees beside her bed and said her prayers. Since Saturday, this day had weighed heavy on her heart. She'd not spoken to Tobit since they'd been at Ezra's, but he was constantly on her mind. She'd woken up thinking she wasn't going with him, but now she was on the fence again.

*He wanted her to be there,* a small voice in the back of her head reminded herself as she rose and dressed. Downstairs, Cora found Eleanor in the kitchen; she was always up first. The room smelled of strong, aromatic coffee, something sweet baking in the oven and fragrant pine boughs decorated with red holly berries Jane had hung in festive swags over the doors and windows.

*"Guder mariye,"* Cora greeted, pouring herself a cup.

"Good morning." Eleanor sat at the table and sipped from a big red mug. Jane had bought a set of red and green mugs on sale that she intended everyone to enjoy through Epiphany before she packed them away until the following year. She tapped the table in front of the chair catty-corner to her. "Want to sit a minute before our hectic day begins?"

"Sure." Cora carried her coffee to the table. "What are you baking?"

"Orange cranberry muffins. Some for us, some for the store to go with the fancy cups of coffee Jane's selling." She sipped her black coffee. "She has quite the head for business. After the first of the year, she wants to start experimenting with making meals and packaging them up for customers to carry home for a homemade supper."

Cora added a bit of cream to her coffee from a glass pitcher on the table. Seasoned cherry burned in the woodstove and the sweet scent mingled with the others in the kitchen.

"Going to school today, I suppose?" Eleanor asked casually.

Cora felt her body tense. "*Ya*, why wouldn't I?"

Eleanor closed a crossword puzzle book she'd been working on. "You decided not to go to Millersville?"

Cora sat back in her chair. Had she made the right decision?

Eleanor held up her hands. "I'm only asking."

Cora leaned forward to rest her elbows on the table, unsure of herself now. "I don't know what to do. A part of me says to stay out of it. If he brings Aida home, I shouldn't be in the van with them."

"*Ya*, but if she isn't coming home. *Ever.* Will you feel guilty that you didn't go when he asked?" Eleanor peered over the brim of her mug.

Cora thought her decision was made but now she

felt flustered. "I don't know," she answered honestly. "Probably yes, but if she wants to come to Honeycomb, I wonder if being there will help me move beyond my feelings for Tobit."

"I can't say for sure," Eleanor answered. "Each of us is different and deals with difficulties in various ways. But hearing you put it that way, maybe it would help. You have to also take into consideration the idea that he might find her and she might want nothing to do with him. Eventually, that could lead to something for you and Tobit."

"I'm trying to not think about anything like that," Cora admitted. "It seems wrong."

"So are you going or not?"

Cora closed her eyes, impatient with herself. It wasn't like her to be indecisive. She was usually able to make choices and stick by them. "I have school today," she groaned. "If I wanted to go, it's too late to cancel. I couldn't get word to everyone before the van is coming."

"So don't cancel." A timer on the kitchen counter went off and Eleanor went to the stove to pull out the muffins.

Eleanor pulled out a muffin pan and then a second. "I wouldn't advise that." She began to pull each muffin from its cup and placed it on a wire rack on the counter to cool.

"*Oll recht*, then what would I do?" Cora asked peevishly.

"Why not let your big sister teach your classes for the day?"

"I can't let you do that." Cora rose and began to pace the wide-plank floor, her arms crossed. "The children are my responsibility. You don't know how to teach school. It's too much to ask of you."

Eleanor tilted her head. "If I can manage this household, I certainly think I can manage forty-some children for a day. I'm sure your lesson plan is already prepared and well thought out. And I'd have Charlie to help me."

Cora walked to her sister. "You would do that for me?" she asked, close to tears of thanks. She realized now that she needed to go with Tobit today, for him, but also for herself. No matter what the outcome.

"I would do anything for you," Eleanor said.

"But the store. *Our vader.*"

"Jane and Willa can handle the store and I'm sure Beth will be happy to pitch in if need be." Eleanor shrugged. "*Dat* can spend the day with them."

Cora hesitated and then declared, "I'll go, then."

"Where are we going?" their father asked, walking into the kitchen. He wore flannel pajamas that Willa had made for him and sheepskin slippers. The Koffmans didn't usually eat in their bedclothes, but they'd found it was easier to let their *dat* wear them through breakfast. That way, he at least stayed in the house.

Cora poured coffee into a mug for him, ignoring the plural *we*. "I'm going to Lancaster County for the day."

"Ah, that's right. With your beau." He sat in his chair at the head of the table.

"*Dat*, he's not my beau. He's a married man. Remember? I told you that," she said, her voice higher-pitched than normal. Now that the decision had been made, she was nervous.

"*Danki,*" he said as she set the coffee in front of him and moved the sugar bowl and creamer closer. "It will be fine, *dochtah*. Not to worry." He patted her as if she were a child. "I'll go with you."

Cora shook her head adamantly. The only thing she could imagine harder than making this journey today would be taking her father with her. "You can't go with me, *Dat. Nay*, absolutely not."

At seven forty-five, Cora watched a white van pull into the parking lot of the Koffman store. She already had her cloak and black bonnet on. She turned to her father, who stood beside her. She wrapped his hand-knit scarf around his neck and handed him his black, wide-brimmed wool hat. "Ready?" she asked him.

He beamed. "Ready!"

*"Goot."* Then she called nervously over her shoulder to Elden and Millie, "Van's here!"

Elden picked up Millie's knitting bag and a small cooler with drinks in it for the ride to Pennsylvania and back. As Millie and her husband walked toward the door, Jane followed, pouting.

"I don't understand why *Dat* can go and I can't." Jane kissed their father's weathered cheek. "I don't say that to be mean, *Dadi*, but you know how trouble is always at your heels."

Their father peered into his youngest daughter's face and laughed. He was having a good morning. He knew all his daughter's names and he remembered that his wife had passed. "True enough, but I keep things interesting around this farm, don't I?" He followed Elden and Millie out the door.

Jane walked beside Cora. "Why can't I go?" she whined. "I've never been to Millersville."

"This isn't a holiday road trip," Cora answered, becoming more nervous as she made her way closer to the van...and Tobit. What would he say when he saw her? Was he angry that she hadn't given him an answer? Would he still want her to go? "Besides, you weren't invited." At the door, she hollered to the back where Beth and Willa were preparing the day's fresh soup to sell. "Leaving! See you tonight."

"See you tonight!" the girls returned in unison.

Throwing her winter cloak over her shoulders, Jane raced down the front porch steps to get ahead of Cora. "Please?" she begged. "I can take care of *Dat* and keep him out of everyone's hair."

Gravel crunched under Cora's black snow boots as she strode toward the van. She wondered what Tobit's response would be when he learned that she was accompanying him after all. She carried her large school satchel packed with homework and tests to be graded. She planned to sit in the back of the van alone so she didn't have to worry about awkward conversations with Tobit. Whatever happened today, he would need some time to himself.

"Jane, I am not going to argue with you," Cora said quietly. "You—" She fell silent as the front passenger door of the van opened and Tobit got out.

His gaze met Cora's but he waited to speak until she was closer. "You changed your mind." He sounded relieved. "*Danki*, Cora."

"Eleanor is teaching school today so she can go," Jane explained.

"I heard that!" Elden called good-naturedly as he got into the van behind Millie.

Tobit looked down at Cora. "I'm glad you decided to come," he said soberly. "That was a good idea, having Eleanor substitute. Our students will enjoy a new face."

"She offered," Cora told him.

He held her gaze for a moment and then looked at Jane. "I understand your *vader* is taking a ride with us, too. Elden didn't say you were coming, but it's good to have so many Koffmans at my side. These days, I almost feel like you're family."

Jane stared at Cora, then turned to Tobit. "I know that I'm not supposed to go, but—" She drew herself up as if trying to appear more adult-like. "I'd like to. I don't know if I can be of any help to you during this difficult time, but at least I can keep *Dat* out of your hair."

He smiled kindly. "I don't mind Felty. He's someone I look up to. I hope to be more like him someday when I grow up. And I'd be happy to have you join us."

Jane bounced excitedly. "Is it *oll recht*, Cora? Because if you don't want me to—"

"We're going to support Tobit," Cora interrupted her little sister. "If he wants you to go, then it's up to you whether you go or not. But you better check with Willa and Beth and be sure they won't need you in the store today."

Jane held up a finger to Tobit. "I'll be right back." Then she ran for the front door.

Cora's gaze drifted back to Tobit.

He spoke first. "I'm glad you decided to come, Cora. I know I have no right to say this, but... I need you."

She didn't know what to say, which was likely a blessing because she feared if she spoke right now, she might not be able to keep her emotions at bay. Instead of speaking, she nodded and climbed into the van, pretending not to see him hold out his hand to help her up.

When Cora got in, she saw that Elden, Millie and their *dat* were already in the back seat so she took the middle one. As she buckled in, Jane jumped into the van, clearly excited to make the unexpected trip. Thankfully, the teenager had the manners to not appear too jubilant.

As the driver pulled out of the store parking lot, Cora glanced up to see Tobit watching her. She let him hold her gaze for a moment and then she got to the business of grading papers.

Tobit didn't know what to expect when he arrived at his in-laws. The whole ride north, he, yet again, rolled all the possibilities over in his mind, considering how he would react to each. What if she was at her parents' home waiting for him? What if she wasn't? What if she wanted to return to Honeycomb with him? What if she didn't?

He tried to remember exactly why Aida had said her parents would not attend their wedding or later why she refused to have any contact with them even after the birth of Elijah. He remembered, at the time, thinking the things she had complained about concerning them were petty. Her grievances seemed childish for an adult woman, but he had listened. Later, he'd encouraged her to mend the broken fences and invite them to visit. As a man who had grown up with little family and none but his sister who cared about him, it had seemed foolish not to at least try to connect with them. But after a while, he gave up speaking of the matter because it was clear to him she wouldn't change her mind.

When the driver pulled in front of Peter and Rhoda Moller's small farmhouse with its peeling paint and missing shingles, he recalled Aida often talking about how poor she had been growing up. While the house looked like it could use some sprucing up, the barnyard was neat, and the fallen snow had been shoveled. Like with the barnyard, Tobit found the inside of the house needing repair but as neat as a pin and smelling fresh and clean. When he introduced himself and his traveling companions, the cousins, Mary and John, were more than kind. The moment he saw their faces, though, he knew what he would learn of Aida wouldn't be good.

After offering refreshments that Tobit and the others declined, they were led into a cramped parlor where Aida's parents waited. Cora had suggested she and the others could remain in the kitchen, but Tobit insisted that they meet his in-laws with him. Peter and Rhoda Moller appeared to be in their seventies. They were small and thin and sat side by side on a threadbare sofa. They were both fully dressed in black, their faces sober.

After another round of introductions, Tobit perched on the edge of one of the kitchen chairs carried in to accommodate the guests. He thanked the Mollers for having them. Then he moved right on to why he was there because he didn't feel he could face another hour not knowing where Aida was or how that would affect the rest of his and Elijah's life.

"I'm looking for my wife," Tobit told the couple. "For your daughter, Aida."

Aida's parents looked at each other, and Peter turned

his rheumy gaze to Tobit. "I'm sorry, *sohn*, but she passed."

It seemed at that moment as if all the oxygen in the air was sucked out of the room. The cousins, Elden, Millie, Jane, Cora and even Felty appeared to hold their breath. Tobit had considered this possibility, but he'd thought others were more likely. "She... She's dead?" he said, his voice cracking.

*"Ya,"* Rhoda said, her voice kind. "We're sorry. So sorry."

"We couldn't tell you on the phone," John explained from where he stood in the doorway with his wife. "It didn't seem right."

Tobit hung his head. He heard a clock ticking in the room; a fire crackled in the decrepit woodstove. He briefly feared he might be sick. Aida was dead. "How... when?" he asked when he found his voice.

Rhoda plucked a cloth handkerchief from her sleeve, sniffed and dabbed at her eyes. "Nine years this last summer."

"Nine years?" Tobit repeated, still in disbelief. "But that would mean..." He took a shuddering breath. All these years he had lain in bed at night wondering where she was, and she had been gone? The thought was almost beyond his comprehension. He'd been angry with her for so long—with a dead woman. "It was January, coming up on ten years, last we saw Aida," he told her parents.

"She came to us in late March, early April. Don't know where she was between leaving you and coming to us. We were still living in New York then. She passed in July of that year," Peter explained.

Tobit stared at the thread-worn rug on the floor. "Was…was she living there with you at the time?"

"*Nay*, never spent a single night under our roof." Rhoda's eyes were teary. "We didn't care that she had a car or was wearing English clothes. We begged her to stay with us, to talk with our bishop, but she…she wanted nothing to do with us or our faith. She got a job working at a motel, cleaning rooms. We prayed and prayed for her, but our prayers went unanswered. There was the alcohol." She glanced at her husband as if fearing she had said too much, but then she went on. "She took drugs, too."

"We suspected, but we didn't know," Peter corrected.

"I was her mother. *I* knew," Rhoda murmured.

Tobit couldn't breathe. He inhaled and exhaled but felt light-headed, as if he wasn't getting enough oxygen. "Did…did she die from… Was it the alcohol and drugs?"

Tobit watched as the man took his wife's hand in his, something rarely seen among the Amish of their age. "It was a robbery, the police told us," Peter said, his words bitter. "She worked the motel's front desk where she cleaned rooms."

"A promotion," Rhoda said. "She told me she had gotten a promotion."

"Someone shot her with a gun," Peter went on as if not hearing his wife. "One hundred fifty-seven dollars. That was what they took. And for that, they murdered my only daughter."

"We tried to get word to you, Tobit," Rhoda explained. "We wanted you to know so you could mourn your wife, but we never heard where she lived with you after she was wed. She didn't want us to know. It was the fall after she passed that we were able to get an address, but the letter we wrote to you was returned." The older woman clasped her wrinkled hands together. "She was never happy with the life we gave her. Never content. Nothing was ever enough, no matter what we did or said. That's why we agreed to the arranged marriage without meeting you. It was what she said she wanted, and we thought it would make her happy."

Tobit hung his head, still trying to absorb that not only was Aida dead, but she had been dead for many years. "I'm sorry I've forced you to speak of this. It must be very painful." His eyes watered. "My...our son and I moved that summer after she left. When I realized she wasn't coming back." He glanced up at them. "I tried to contact you after she left. I found your address in things she left behind, but the letter returned address unknown as well."

"We've moved a lot," Peter said. "Rented places. Like this one. Here this year, gone the next."

Tobit covered his eyes with his hand and sniffed. He had so many thoughts and competing emotions that hanging on to a single one was impossible. He felt someone press a handkerchief into his hand and he looked up. It was Cora. Her eyes were brimming with tears. He took the square of cloth, noting the tiny *C* embroidered on the corner of the white cotton before blotting his eyes with it and then his nose.

They didn't stay long in the Mollers' home. There was no need, and Tobit felt that Peter and Rhoda wanted him to go as much as he wanted to leave. Their emotions were too raw. On their porch steps, Tobit thanked

Aida's parents again and promised to be in touch. They seemed eager to meet their grandson, and Tobit promised to figure something out after the first of the year when he had his cast removed.

The moment goodbyes were complete, Elden, Millie, Jane and Felty all rushed to get into the van and away from the pall over the Mollers' home. Only Cora hung back and walked beside him toward the van.

"Oh, Tobit," Cora murmured. "I don't know what to say except that I am so sorry." Never, in her wildest dreams, had she thought Aida could have been dead since a short time after she left him. That meant that he hadn't been lying. He was a widower. She understood, of course, that based on the information he had, he had lied. But somehow the facts made her feel better. She was sorry the poor woman was dead but relieved that she hadn't fallen for a married man.

"There's nothing *to* say," he answered miserably. "First, I had to tell my son that his mother abandoned him. Now I have to tell him that she's dead." He stopped walking. "How am I going to do that?"

"The same way you told him about how she left. I don't know what you said that day, but you must have said it well because he came to school the next day without any indication that anything had happened."

"I have made such a mess of things, of my life, of my son's."

"*Nay*, you haven't made a mess of anything." She surprised herself by grabbing his hand. "As for what you're going to do, you're going to go home to Honeycomb, get a good night's sleep and, in the morning, you'll sit down with Elijah and tell him what the Mollers told you."

"But Elijah knows I came here today looking for her. I have to tell him tonight."

Even though she didn't want to, she released his hand, not wanting anyone else to see them. "But Elijah won't be there tonight. He's staying at our house with Charlie. They're going on the hayride to sing Christmas carols to elderly folks."

"That's right."

"Let's go home," Cora said, indicating the van. "You need time to process what you've learned today and speak with our bishop. And once you get past this, we can talk about ourselves." The moment the words were out of her mouth, she wished she could take them back. How selfish of her to think about her romantic feelings toward him when he'd just received such awful news. "Tobit, I—"

"They're waiting for us," he interrupted. "We should go."

She looked up, hoping to get reassurance that he wasn't angry that she'd been so insensitive, but he refused to meet her gaze. They walked to the van and got in without another word to each other.

## Chapter Fourteen

The Sunday before Christmas, Tobit stood at Matt Beachy's fence dressed all in black except for a white dress shirt. He watched a dozen driving horses mill about in a paddock and wondered when he could escape and go home. Bishop Cyrus's sermon had been long and directed at him, but the man made it clear that forgiveness was there for those who had taken a misstep and were repentant. Before the congregation was adjourned for the midday meal, Tobit stood before his new congregation, confessed his transgressions and vowed to be a better man. It had been easier than he had expected, though by no means pleasant.

After such a stressful day, he was eager to take his leave of the stares, mostly from the Koffman women. It was clear that the family was displeased with him, and it had nothing to do with his deceased wife or the lie he had told. None of them had come out and said it, but he was certain that they all expected him to walk out with Cora once they discovered that he truly was a widower.

He knew Cora had anticipated the same. He saw it in

her eyes the other day when he and Elijah stopped at the Koffman store. Tobit would have rather driven to Byler's in Dover, but the boy had been insistent about buying a pair of sunglasses the Koffmans stocked. Tobit had half hoped she wouldn't be there, but he knew he couldn't avoid her and her family forever. He had taken her by surprise; she was stocking shelves. He'd said hello but hadn't initiated any conversation and she hadn't, either.

Today he'd caught her watching him at church service several times. With the men and women seated separately, women on one side of the aisle, men on the other, it was hard to miss when a woman stared at you. In her eyes, he saw pain and disappointment, and it made him miserable to think that he couldn't give her what she wanted. Maybe Cora hadn't thought he should come courting so soon after news of his wife, but he sensed that she wanted an expression of his commitment to her. But how could he do that after the way he had failed Aida and then Elijah?

"Wondered where you got to," a voice behind Tobit said.

He glanced over his shoulder. It was Elden, who to his word had stood beside him through the whole Aida ordeal.

Elden leaned on the fence. "You did well today in your confession. I'd hope if I ever have to do that, I can do it half as well as you."

"I suppose I should say thank you," Tobit responded as he stared at the long row of black buggies on the far side of the paddock. "But thanking someone for their compliment on how well you stand in front of fifty-odd people and tell them you sinned doesn't sit well with me."

"But it's over now and no one has any doubt that you regret your choices." Elden glanced at him. They were both shivering despite wearing heavy black coats over their Sunday clothes. The weather had turned bitterly cold. "And now it's time to move on. Before you know it, Christmas will be here and you'll be back behind your desk at school after the first of the year."

"And Cora will no longer have a job," Tobit observed quietly. The idea of moving had again occurred to him. If he and Elijah relocated to a place where no one knew them or their story, he could honestly say he was widowed without having to provide any background to his story. And if he gave up his position at the Clover school, Cora could keep the job.

"You talk to her since we went to Millersville?"

"We ran into her at the store the other day."

"I don't mean did you chat about the weather. I mean, have you *talked* with her? That was a brave thing she did, paying a call to your in-laws. For all she knew, for all any of us did, your wife could have been there waiting for you. She knew that but sacrificed her feelings to be there for you."

"Don't you think I know that?" Tobit grumbled. He thrust his cold hands into his coat pockets and stared at the horses.

Elden turned to face him and rested one foot on the bottom rung of the fence. "I can't imagine how it must feel to have gone through all this, Tobit. But I think you've come out the other side. The worst is behind you, and you should start looking for the best. I can't begin to see what was in God's plan in how this all unfolded with your wife, but today you have a door to a different life. You've confessed, and you're free of your sin. I hope you don't close that door."

*Meaning he should marry Cora?* Fearing he might say something unkind to his friend, who had been nothing but good to him, Tobit kept his mouth shut.

"Look, I'm not telling you that you should walk out with Cora." He shrugged. "Maybe the feelings we all thought you had for her aren't there any longer. There's nothing wrong with that. I know you both need to find a spouse, but you deserve to love and be loved. If you don't love her or see love for her in your future, that's *oll recht*. But you need to have that hard conversation with Cora."

"So you've been talking about me with her?" Tobit tried to keep his tone neutral. He didn't want to be that man who took out his frustrations with himself on others. He glanced at the overcast sky to avoid eye contact with Elden.

"I have not, not directly, at least."

"Ah, Millie."

Elden sighed. "It's the kind of things husbands and wives talk about. I'm glad Millie feels she can discuss her concerns with me. But I would never say anything to anyone else about what she and I have discussed concerning you and her sister."

A long moment of silence ticked by. Then another. Tobit knew Elden was waiting for him to continue the conversation, but he didn't have it in him today. The confession in front of the church had his emotions in turmoil. Instead, he said, "I'm going to round up Elijah and head home. Good to see you." He walked away.

"At least think about what I said," Elden called after him.

Tobit raised his hand in acknowledgment but didn't turn around.

"And we'll see you at the Christmas program at school, if not before," Elden hollered.

This time, Tobit pretended not to hear him.

Cora arranged eight Christmas-tree-shaped sugar cookies on a wire rack and slid it to Millie. It was a little after one o'clock on Christmas Eve and the Koffman sisters had closed the store early for the holiday weekend. While the women had handled a steady stream of customers, Cora had spent the last two hours in the kitchen baking enough cookies so that each of her students would have one. She was making an individual gift bag for each of them, including a giant cookie with their name on it.

The only problem with the plan was that she miscalculated how much time it would take to shop for and put the bags together. And she'd waited too long to make the cookies. She had to be at the school by four thirty to get the woodstove going and ensure that everything was in place for their guests' arrival at five forty-five. Parents would bring cookies for refreshments after the program, but she also planned to offer hot and cold apple cider. She would heat cider in a soup pot on the woodstove and add cinnamon and nutmeg, which would make the schoolroom smell even better than it already did with all the pine greenery the children had used for decorations. There were homemade Christmas cards, posters and loops of red and green paper chains, which added to the festive atmosphere.

That morning she'd risen at five, intending to work on the cookies immediately. However, she woke exhausted. She'd lain in bed for hours vacillating between worrying about whether the Christmas program would be successful and what to do about Tobit. Now she wished she'd had more coffee; she would need it if she wanted to stay awake that evening.

*"Oll recht,"* Cora said to her sisters. "You each have a bag of green icing. All you have to do is frost them as you see fit so they look like Christmas trees. There are also bags of white and brown icing if you want to add any details. And the red—" she pointed to the decorator bag "—is to write the student's name. You each have a list of the eight students you're making them for. This doesn't have to be fancy," she told them as she moved her rack of cookies closer. "Oh, and there are also sprinkles."

The back door banged open, and two boys entered in heavy barn coats, gloves and black ski masks so you couldn't see their faces. Charlie and Elijah. Elijah had spent the night again. Charlie had been careful not to reveal confidences, but Cora got the idea that Elijah was trying to avoid his father. From what she could gather from others, Tobit had been a bear since their return from Millersville.

Cora had returned to Honeycomb sad for Tobit and Elijah but unable to suppress the tiny spark of excitement that they would be free to pursue their attraction to each other when he was ready. She had expected he wouldn't be ready to date immediately, but it hadn't occurred to her that he wouldn't want to see her. He had made no attempt since he learned of his wife's passing and Cora was baffled by his behavior toward her. He hadn't come to the school or sought her out at home and avoided her at church earlier in the week.

The Englishers had a word for his behavior. He was *ghosting* her. She'd heard two young women in the store talking about a boy ghosting one of them by ignoring her texts and phone calls after they'd been dating. She and Tobit hadn't been dating, but she had no doubt he had been attracted to her because that precipitated his confession. Now that he had learned that his wife had died years before, she had expected they would have a conversation about their feelings for each other. She didn't expect a commitment or a timeline so soon, but she was disappointed and heartbroken that he'd been completely avoiding her.

She must have misread his attraction to her. That was the only reasonable explanation. He'd enjoyed the flirting because he knew he was married and nothing could ever come of it. He'd only been interested in her when he was unavailable.

Charlie pulled off his mask. "Can we make some hot chocolate with the fancy machine out front? I want to show Elijah."

Elijah pulled off his mask, avoiding eye contact with Cora.

"*Ya*, but no boots," Jane told them as she outlined one of the cookies in green frosting. "Leave them by the door. I just swept and mopped out front."

The sisters all put their attention on the cookies, and

it wasn't until the boys had left with big paper cups of hot chocolate that Millie brought up what had to be on everyone's mind that hadn't been said.

She glanced at Cora standing beside her. "I feel bad for Elijah. He's got enough dealing with what he's learned about his mother, but then to have Tobit avoiding you." She shook her head. "Charlie said that Elijah misses you."

Cora smiled sadly. She had no idea how good a mother she could be to a teenager but felt she'd grown close to the boy and would miss him.

"I know there has to be a mourning time for the wife," Jane said, "but I thought Tobit liked you, Cora."

"We all did," Willa agreed. "But like I said, plenty of single men out there. Ones not so complicated."

Cora felt her eyes tear up.

"You should talk to him, make him talk to you," Beth advised, her tone kind. "At least then you'll know where you stand."

Cora shook her head. "I already told you, told everyone. If he doesn't want to speak to me, that's fine. I'm fine."

"You are not fine," Millie insisted impatiently. "You're miserable, and the silly thing about all of this is that he is, too. Honestly, I can't decide which of you is more stubborn. You make me want to take matters into my own hands and talk to him myself."

"Don't you dare, Millie," Cora flared. "This is between the two of us."

"Then *talk* to each other," Millie insisted.

"How about a different subject." Cora picked up the sleeve of white frosting to add snow to the tips of her cookie tree branches. "It's Christmas Eve," she said, trying to sound festive even when she didn't feel it. "Let's sing some Christmas songs. It will get us in the spirit for tonight's school program."

It didn't go unnoticed by Cora that before Millie began to sing "We Three Kings," the sisters all exchanged glances as if a conspiracy was at hand.

*Great,* Cora thought. *Now what do I have to worry about?*

As Cora stood at the back of the schoolhouse listening to Elijah sing solo the last song of the evening, she realized she'd had nothing to worry about as far as the Christmas program. The students had memorized the Bible verses they recited and remembered every word of the songs. Except for Apple Detweiler, of course, but her angelic, slightly off-key voice had been one of the best performances of the evening, bringing tears to the eyes of many a friend and neighbor.

The school was packed not just with parents and grandparents of her students, but it seemed as if half of Honeycomb had turned out for the last school program scheduled for the Christmas season. Cora didn't know if they'd come to see if she'd been successful in planning the annual event or if they were there to observe Tobit. By now, the story of his wife and him had been spoken of in every quilting circle and line at Raber's Feed Store. She wasn't sure which reason she preferred for the impressive turnout, but it didn't matter. What mattered was that it was the eve of Christ's birth. She was thankful for the gift of *Gott's* son and for the loving family and community she had. Sadly, the romance she had hoped for hadn't materialized, but she told herself she would be okay. She would be okay…if not a little sadder.

As Charlie joined Elijah in the last stanza of "Come All Ye Faithful," a lump rose in her throat. After the first of the year, Tobit would return to his position and she would no longer be a teacher. In the middle of the night, it had occurred to her that if Honeycomb didn't want women teachers, maybe an Amish community elsewhere would. Perhaps she needed a change of scenery, as Englishers liked to say. She had second cousins in Indiana who were female and taught school. One even continued to teach after she married. Maybe in a place like that, she mused, she could get a job teaching and start anew. A place far from Tobit.

As Charlie and Elijah reached the end of the song, they encouraged their guests to join in on one more chorus and the sounds of the voices, young and old, made Cora's heart swell. She would be sad to leave her students. They'd taught her as much as she'd taught them in their short time together. But she was proud of what she had done in the past two months.

When the song ended, one of the district's deacons closed the program with a prayer and then Cora invited everyone to enjoy the refreshments. As she moved through the crowd, accepting compliments and well-meaning suggestions, she looked for Tobit. Each time she located him, it seemed like he had just looked away from her. Yet when she moved in his direction while hugging a student or exchanging Christmas well-wishes with a friend, he moved, putting more distance between them.

Once every Christmas cookie, brownie and slice of cake had been eaten and every drop of apple cider drunk, folks began to gather their children and head home. As Cora cleaned up, bagging trash and moving desks and chairs, she chatted with her sisters and others who had stayed back to help. Tobit was one of the men who remained behind, but he stayed clear of her, directing others and acting as if it was his school again. Which it was.

Cora fought a wave of sadness as she swept the floor. Once she checked the embers in the woodstove, she'd be ready to go. Eleanor, the other Koffmans and Beth and her husband, Jack, had taken the family buggy but Millie and Elden had promised to give her a ride home.

"Looks like we're just about done here," Millie called from the doorway to the cloakroom. "I'll see if he's ready. I think he and Tobit are checking to see how much firewood is here and whether any needs to be delivered between Christmas and the start of the new year."

"I'll be out directly," Cora said and turned her back on her sister to return to sweeping.

Cora heard Millie leave, then the door opened again, and a cold blast of air whooshed into the room. She heard a man's slow footfall and realized who it had to be by the limping gait. She froze, gripping the broom handle. No one else was inside but the two of them. Was this Tobit's way of getting a moment to speak with her privately? As she swept the dirt into a dustpan, she sneaked a peek at him. He'd brought in more firewood so he would have dry wood on the first day of the new semester when the children returned from their vacation.

Tobit stacked the wood, and as she carried the dirt to a trash can, he walked toward the cloakroom to go. He never looked at her.

Cora's heart sank.

"Gonna head out if there's nothing else you need," he said.

"That's it, *danki*." She forced a smile and tried to keep her voice steady. "Enjoy your day tomorrow. *Hallicher Grischtdaag*."

"Merry Christmas," he replied.

Cora put the broom and dustpan away, banked the coals in the woodstove, blew out the gas lamps and switched off the solar-powered lights. Eager to get home and into her bed, she put on her cloak, tied a woolen scarf around her neck and tied her black bonnet over her prayer *kapp*. Grabbing her wool gloves, she checked for her keys in her pocket, turned off the battery lamp, stepped outside and pulled the door, locking it behind her.

As she slipped her hands into her wool gloves, she watched Tobit's buggy turn out of the school's driveway and onto the road, headed for home. The next thing she saw…or, more importantly, *didn't* see, was Elden and Millie's buggy. She walked down the steps, looking around to the back to be sure she hadn't missed them, but there were no buggies. Everyone was gone. But that made no sense. Millie had said she was going outside to see if Elden was ready to head home. She and Beth had come early together in Beth's buggy with Jack catching a ride to the schoolhouse with the Koffman family later. Beth, Jack and Charlie had, however, left right after the program ended to join the Lehmans for family prayer. Cora was supposed to ride home with Millie and Elden—that had been the plan.

Cora took the steps and stood in the dead grass. *Her family had forgotten her?* They had left her, she thought in astonishment. There was certainly confusion with so many people there tonight, but how could they have forgotten her? Left her here alone? She was the reason they'd all been there tonight!

Then she realized she wasn't alone. Before he stepped out of the shadows, she recognized the tall, broad-shouldered figure. It was Tobit. She looked from him to the road and back at him. She could still hear the metal horseshoes striking the pavement as his horse and buggy drove away.

"Wasn't that your buggy that just left?" she asked in confusion.

"*Ya.*" He sounded annoyed, bordering on angry. "And I don't see your buggy. Elden and Millie just pulled out and went the other way."

Cora stared at the dark. "Then who drove your—"

"Elijah," he said, not waiting to hear her question. "That was him driving." He looked at her. "It seems my son stole my buggy. And your family left you. On Christmas Eve."

"But why would they—" Cora didn't finish her sentence as their gazes met. "Ah," she said.

"Ah, indeed," he agreed.

# Chapter Fifteen

Cora stared at Tobit. She was tired and her brain was sluggish. "I understand how I could have been left behind," she said slowly. "There was the usual confusion with my family when they headed out, and we came in different buggies than we were supposed to leave in. But there are only two of you in your house. How did Elijah forget you?"

Tobit slowly walked toward her. "I don't think my *sohn* forgot me, nor do I think Elden and Millie forgot you."

The frigid night air was clearing her head. "Why would—" Then it hit her. She felt herself blush. "They left us here on purpose."

"To force us to be alone together," he said, walking toward the road.

"To talk." Cora wrapped her arms around herself, shivering, and followed him. At the edge of the driveway, she looked in both directions. The taillights of the buggies were far in the distance. "How dare they," she muttered, although she didn't have enough energy to work up any anger. "But it's *oll recht*. It's not far from home. I can just walk." She looked at him. "But you shouldn't walk half a mile home, should you? We could unlock the school and you could wait where it's warm. I'll go home and get a buggy and— *Nay*, that doesn't make sense. Why don't I walk to your house, get your buggy and bring it back. Then you can drive me home. Or Elijah, if you prefer."

Tobit turned to her and stared. "You really would do that for me, wouldn't you?" he asked, his voice sounding strange.

She made herself look at him. "Of course I would."

He sighed. "Oh, Cora…"

The tenderness of his tone when he spoke her name made her heart skip a beat. So he did care for her. She had not imagined it. He had cared for her and still did.

"Cora, you know me. Do you think I would let you walk home so I could ride?"

"But your broken leg." She pointed.

"In a week the cast will be removed and I'll have no restrictions." He lifted his chin in the direction of his house. "Come on, let's walk back to my place. I'll get the buggy and take you home."

"Do you really think you should go so far?" she protested weakly, feeling nervous. She'd wanted to talk to Tobit since they returned from Millersville, but she was afraid. She feared what he might say or not say.

"Cora, they're right. We do need to talk." He stepped onto the pavement facing the direction home. "So we can either talk standing here freezing, or we can walk and talk and warm up a bit. What will it be?"

Not trusting her voice, she joined him on the road

and fell into step beside him. For a short distance, they were both quiet. Only the echoes of their footfall, the scurry of small creatures in the woods along the road and the occasional hoot of an owl could be heard. The air was cold, the clouds dark overhead. It smelled like snow, which surprised her because there had been no prediction for a white Christmas.

"I'm sorry that I've been such a coward," he finally said.

"Coward?" She frowned. "How could anyone think you're a coward? You didn't have to confess to the church. Or you could have at least stalled it. Or you could have moved again and joined a new Amish community and no one would probably have ever known your circumstances. But you didn't do that, Tobit. You stayed here and you faced your mistakes."

"I thought about moving," he told her.

"You did?" She drew back, then confessed, "I did, too."

"You thought about moving? Leaving your family?"

She nodded.

"Because of me?"

"Yes and no. Mostly because of me. Look, Tobit…" She hesitated. There was no way to say this but to be vulnerable to him and to say it. "I know you never made a promise to me. We've never gone on a date or held hands, but—" Her voice caught in her throat. "But I thought you cared for me and I… I care for you, Tobit. But all that's my own doing," she continued. "I have no right to expect anything from you. It was my girlish misinterpretation of our working relationship that—"

"Don't have a right?" he interrupted. "Of course you do, Cora. I've treated you terribly. I thought I was still legally married, yet I allowed myself to have feelings for you. I allowed you to feel things for me." They walked so close together that the sleeve of his coat brushed her cloak. "As a married man, no matter how long Aida had been gone, I had no right to do that. But I was lonely and—and I didn't even know I was until I met you." He exhaled. "I'm sorry for that."

*"Danki,"* she said, trying to wrap her head around what he was saying. So she *hadn't* imagined his feelings for her. "I accept your apology," she said. "But what happened after you found out she had passed? After we returned from Pennsylvania? I knew you needed some time to think about all that had happened, but I was sure you would come to me and we could talk." She halted on the road and looked at him. Despite the dark clouds in the sky, a half-moon was rising in the eastern sky, illuminating the path to Tobit's home. And now illuminating his handsome face. "I thought we had become close. Why didn't you come to me?"

"Because you deserve a better man than me," he explained. "Cora, you are such a good woman, kind and smart and full of faith. You're too good for me, for a man who has sinned as I have."

To her surprise, Cora laughed aloud. "I thought you only liked me because you weren't available, and nothing could ever come of it."

"You thought *what*?" he demanded. "What kind of man do you think I am, Cora? I would never do that to someone. Certainly not to you. I didn't come to you because I felt guilty. I lied and said my wife was dead when I knew no such thing. What kind of man does that to his wife? To his son?"

She faced him squarely. "Tobit, you made a mistake. You never meant to harm anyone. You did it for Elijah. Wrong or not, your heart was in the right place. And now you've confessed and been forgiven."

He looked down at her. "I have been forgiven by *Gott*, haven't I?" he asked quietly. "And I suppose redemption is only true redemption if it's used for good in the world." He gazed down at her small gloved hands in his. "I guess my question to you, Cora, is can you forgive me? For all of it. For taking your job."

She felt giddy. He liked her! She *hadn't* imagined it. "You did not take my job," she told him firmly. "It was my mistake to believe that. Those men never had any intention of hiring me."

He shook his head. "Well, I'm still sorry for not coming to you to tell you how unworthy I've felt since our trip. I had the confession hanging over my head and Elijah to worry about and…and forgive me. Please?"

She smiled up at him, her heart beating fast. "I can do that."

"And can you…" He squeezed her hands. "Do you think you could find it in your heart to give me a second chance? I think we should wait sometime before we make it official, but… Would you walk out with me?"

When she gazed up at him, she saw the first snowflakes drifting down from the sky. "*Ya.* I will."

He threw his arms around her and held her in a hug like none other she had ever experienced. Standing in the falling snow, Tobit's embrace made her feel warm and safe and full of hope for a future together she had never dreamed of.

# *Epilogue*

*Five Months Later*
*Clover School*
*Honeycomb, Delaware*

Jane walked into the schoolhouse. "There you are!"

"Here I am." Standing at a desk, Cora held up a wool scarf in one hand and a bag of marbles in the other. "I'm going through the lost-and-found box. I thought I'd put the stuff outside on a table. If the students don't know what belongs to them, maybe their parents will."

"That's nice of you to do that. It's not even your school anymore."

Cora shrugged, "*Ya*, but you know men don't think to do this sort of thing. If I don't do something with this box, Tobit will still have it when school begins again in September."

"Tobit." Jane pointed at her sister. "That's why I was looking for you. He's looking for you. He's out back at the swings fixing one of the seats before the children arrive."

They were having a picnic and students and parents would soon descend upon the little schoolhouse. They would have a potluck meal to welcome in the summer and say goodbye to another school year. There would be foot and sack races, tossing games and a short program by the children, including several songs, thanks to Elijah's insistence. While Tobit hadn't wanted to organize the day, he'd been happy to let Cora do it. He'd also been so busy over the last few days that he'd been thankful to have her grade papers for him. It wasn't the same as teaching the classes alone, but she enjoyed assisting Tobit and helping the students improve.

Jane plucked the marbles and scarf from her big sister's hands. "I'll go through this stuff and put it on a table for folks to claim. Go see what your bear wants."

Cora pressed her lips together in a giggle. She would never call him that to his face, but Tobit *was* her bear now and all her sisters referred to him that way when they were alone. Cora and Tobit had been walking out together for months and were now accepted in the community as a couple. If anyone held any animosity toward Tobit for his past transgressions, she hadn't heard about it. It was interesting how Honeycomb could be such a hive of gossip when it came to little things, but in serious matters like his, folks easily found it in their hearts to forgive, forget and embrace their lost sheep.

"What does he want?" Cora asked.

Jane rolled her eyes as if to say she had no idea and Cora walked out of the schoolhouse and into the bright sunshine of late May. The school board members were already there, setting up tables to serve the food. Folks would bring blankets and they would all dine picnic-style. Just as Jane had said, she found Tobit at the swing set. He was putting his tools into a big plastic bucket he carried them in.

"Hey," she called to him.

He glanced up and grinned and Cora felt all warm and fluttery inside. The last months with Tobit hadn't always been perfect. They'd had their share of disagreements, but she had gone from fearing she might be falling in love with him to loving him without abandon. And she knew he felt the same way about her because he told her all the time that he loved her.

"You were looking for me?"

"I was." He grasped the leather seat of the swing. "Hop on and let's see if I fixed this thing."

She frowned, staring at the swing. "Really? You want me to swing in front of the students? I'll never hear the end of it from them or the adults."

"Oh, come on. You always tell me I need to step outside my box. Maybe you do, too." He glanced around. "No one is even here yet to see you."

She pursed her mouth, eyeing him. "The school board?"

He waved away her concern. "They can't even see us. Come on. It will be fun and I have something to talk to you about. Two things, actually."

*"Oll recht,"* she said, looking at him suspiciously. But she sat in the swing and grasped the ropes it hung from.

He gave her a push. "I just talked to the school board members and it's been decided that rather than building a new schoolhouse nearby to accommodate the families moving to Honeycomb, a second room will be built onto this building."

"Really?" she asked with a grin, glancing over her shoulder at him. He pushed her again and she flew through the air. "That's wonderful news!"

"I suppose," he grumbled. "But that will mean more students for me. More papers to grade."

"True," she agreed, thinking about how that *would* complicate matters. She'd learned when she'd been teaching that while most days a well-organized person could manage forty children, she couldn't imagine having more. "But I know you'll make it work, Tobit. And you can call on the older children to help."

He pushed her again and the breeze against her face was exhilarating.

"I was thinking," Tobit continued, "that I need a bit more help than that, so…" When she flew back, he pushed her again. "I've told the board they have to hire you for next school year. Otherwise, I won't renew my contract."

"You what?" Cora was so excited that she jumped into the air and landed on her feet. "Oh, Tobit. And they agreed?"

He shrugged his broad shoulders. "I don't think they felt they had much choice."

Her heart pounded. She couldn't believe she was going to get to teach again. And this time, Tobit would be at her side. She already knew they would make a great team. *"Danki,"* she whispered, wishing she could throw herself into his arms. But with the school board members milling around, she wouldn't want them to see her and think her unprofessional. Instead, she satisfied herself by gazing into his gorgeous blue eyes. "Wow. I can't believe it," she mused aloud. She glanced at him. "Was there something else?"

"There is, but not here." He grabbed her hand and pulled her after him. His leg had healed completely, and he no longer even limped.

Cora laughed, feeling giddy and just a little naughty. "What are you doing? This is entirely inappropriate, Teacher."

He led her behind the schoolhouse, out of view of the others. "I need to ask you something, Teacher," he said when they were alone and shielded by the building.

Her head was already full of plans for the new school year. Would she and Tobit divide the children, with her taking the younger ones and him taking the older ones? Or would they each teach different subjects? She didn't know the best way to do it, because most Amish schools only had one teacher. But she was certain they would be able to figure out together the best approach.

"What did you want to ask?" she said. "I still have a few things to do before everyone arrives."

Facing her, he took both her hands. "I've never done this before," he murmured, suddenly seeming nervous.

She looked up at him. "Done what?"

He took a deep breath. "I spoke to Bishop Cyrus last night and your father and…we're all on the same page. It's time for me to move on with my life, so…"

He took another breath and Cora wondered what he was trying to say. Usually he was so confident and— and then she realized where he was going with this and her eyes filled with tears of joy.

"Cora Koffman, will you marry me?" he blurted.

She gazed up at him, unable to stop smiling. She crooked her finger, signaling for him to lean down to hear her. "I will marry you, Tobit," she whispered. And then, in a bold move, she raised up on her toes and they shared their very first kiss. The first of many.

\* \* \* \* \*

Dear Reader,

Thank you for joining me in the Old Order Amish community of Honeycomb, Delaware again. I hope you're enjoying getting to know the seven Koffman sisters. I love the way each of the young women is finding herself while remaining true to her faith.

I'm so glad that Cora was able to set aside her resentment of Tobit long enough to see the man for who he was and who he could be. Had it not been for Tobit's love for Cora, I wonder if he would have found the courage to admit his failings to himself and others. Even if things hadn't worked out between him and Cora, I think he would have felt a sense of peace with the admission of his mistakes. I'm so glad they found love in the end, though!

Now that Millie, Beth and Cora have found husbands, my next story will focus on Henrietta. What kind of man will it take to convince her to settle down? I hope you'll join me next year to find out.

Blessings,
*Emma Miller*

# COMING NEXT MONTH FROM
## Love Inspired

### AN UNUSUAL AMISH WINTER MATCH
*Indiana Amish Market* • by Vannetta Chapman

With his crops failing, Amish bachelor Ethan King already has enough problems. He certainly doesn't need flighty Ada Yoder adding to his troubles. But when a family emergency requires them to work together, they'll discover that the biggest problem isn't their differences—it's their feelings for each other.

### BONDING OVER THE AMISH BABY
by Pamela Desmond Wright

After a car accident, Dr. Caleb Sutter is stranded in a Texas Amish community. Then he suddenly becomes the temporary guardian to a newborn, along with pretty Amish teacher Rebecca Schroder. But the baby soon raises questions about his family history, leading Caleb to a crossroads between his past—and a future love...

### THE COWBOY'S CHRISTMAS COMPROMISE
*Wyoming Legacies* • by Jill Kemerer

Recently divorced Dalton Cambridge can't afford to turn down a ranch manager position—even if the boss is his ex-wife's new husband's ex-wife. Besides, working for Erica Black is strictly business. But when he finds himself caring for the single mother, will he risk everything for a holiday family?

### THEIR HOLIDAY SECRET
by Betsy St. Amant

Preston Green will do anything for a fake girlfriend—even bid on one at a charity auction. Lulu Boyd is the perfect choice to stop his mother's matchmaking. And it's just for one holiday family dinner. Soon it feels all too real...but another secret might make this their last Christmas together.

### A COUNTRY CHRISTMAS
by Lisa Carter

Kelsey Summerfield is thrilled to plan her grandfather's upcoming wedding. But the bride's grandson, Clay McKendry, is determined to keep the city girl's ideas in check. When a series of disasters threaten to derail the big day, will they put aside their differences...and find their own happily-ever-after?

### THE DOCTOR'S CHRISTMAS DILEMMA
by Danielle Thorne

Once upon a time, Ben Cooper left town to become a big-city doctor. Now he's back to run his father's clinic and spend Christmas with his daughter. Not to fall for old love McKenzie Price. But when McKenzie helps Ben reconnect with his little girl, will Ben accept this second chance at love?

---

**LOOK FOR THESE AND OTHER LOVE INSPIRED BOOKS WHEREVER BOOKS ARE SOLD, INCLUDING MOST BOOKSTORES, SUPERMARKETS, DISCOUNT STORES AND DRUGSTORES.**

LICNM0923

# Get 3 FREE REWARDS!

**We'll send you 2 FREE Books <u>plus</u> a FREE Mystery Gift.**

**FREE**
Value Over
**$20**

Both the **Love Inspired** and **Love Inspired** Suspense series feature compelling novels filled with inspirational romance, faith, forgiveness and hope.

# HARLEQUIN
## PLUS

Try the best multimedia subscription service for romance readers like you!

---

## Read, Watch and Play.

Experience the easiest way to get the romance content you crave.

Start your **FREE TRIAL** at
<u>www.harlequinplus.com/freetrial</u>.